The Farther You Run

Davida
Wills
Hurwin

VIKING

Also by **Davida Wills Hurwin**

A Time for Dancing

VIKING

Published by Penguin Group
Penguin Young Readers Group, 345 Hudson Street, New York, New York 10014, U.S.A.
Penguin Books Ltd, 80 Strand, London WC2R 0RL, England
Penguin Books Australia Ltd, 250 Camberwell Road, Camberwell, Victoria 3124, Australia
Penguin Books Canada Ltd, 10 Alcorn Avenue, Toronto, Ontario, Canada M4V 3B2
Penguin Books (N.Z.) Ltd, 182-190 Wairau Road, Auckland 10, New Zealand

Published in 2003 by Viking, a division of Penguin Young Readers Group

1 3 5 7 9 10 8 6 4 2

LIBRARY OF CONGRESS CATALOGING-IN-PUBLICATION DATA

Hurwin, Davida, date-
The farther you run / Davida Wills Hurwin.
p. cm.
Summary: Even with a new best friend and a new boyfriend, Samantha has a
hard time adjusting to life without her best friend Juliana, who died of cancer.
ISBN 0-670-03627-7
[1. Grief—Fiction. 2. Death—Fiction. 3. Best friends—Fiction.
4. Friendship—Fiction.] I. Title.
PZ7.H95735Far 2003   [Fic]—dc21   2003000951

Printed in U.S.A.
Set in Berkeley

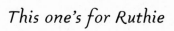
This one's for Ruthie

Part ONE

~

"No more questions, please . . ."

All lyrics are from *Into the Woods*
by Stephen Sondheim

Mona

Turning nineteen wasn't quite what I'd hoped for. In fact, it sucked. Not that I expected my problems to magically sort themselves out, but—hello! When you're one year away from twenty, you should at least have *some* control of your life. The best *I* could manage was a part-time job at Mickey D's. I still lived with my mother, I didn't have a car, and in a whole year of serving Happy Meals, I had not managed to save one penny. Then there was the situation with the diploma. Did it really matter that I flunked English in my senior year? I passed it every other time. Why not give me the stupid piece of paper so I could find a job that paid something? But no, *I* had to go to summer school. The fact that it started on my birthday didn't surprise me in the least.

My first class was at eight, an ungodly time to be coherent, especially in summer, *and* it was held at the junior college, which meant no parking, anywhere. That didn't affect me so much, since my mother had changed her mind just that morning and told me that no, I would not be using her car. Like she promised.

She dropped me off five minutes late and with a pissy little smile, told me to take the bus home. When I finally found the stupid room, the place was packed. The professor, who, if she ever had sex probably did it to herself, sat behind her little pulpit, plotting our immediate future, no doubt gloating that several of us couldn't find desks to sit in.

After this, I could look forward to typing class. Wow. What a birthday celebration.

We'd just started the lecture about the reading list, with me wondering how the hell I'd do it all in six weeks, when someone came running up the stairs. The entire class turned as the door slammed open against the wall.

Miss America stood there, lean, long-haired, long-legged, beautiful and—what else?—blonde. She struck a pose, one hand on her hip, the other holding onto the doorway, and smiled.

"Well, shit. Am I late?" She focused on the professor, whose little prude mouth puckered even tighter. "Sorry," she said, with a shrug that plainly said she wasn't. "No parking."

"Everyone else seemed to find a place," Prof sniffed, "Miss . . . ?"

"Russell. Samantha Russell. Really, I—"

"Please sit down, Miss Russell." Prof made a great show of marking down something in her grade book. The girl nodded and then looked around the room.

"Okay, but there's no—"

"Perhaps tomorrow you'll be on time." Prof turned back to the board and scribbled even faster. Her big old butt wiggled as she wrote. The new girl shook her head, smiling in this what-the-hell-is-*your*-problem kinda way. I smiled, too, hiding it behind my hand. I didn't particularly want to, but I liked her. Partly because the professor *didn't*, partly because she was severely beautiful and didn't act like God's gift. Mostly because she obviously didn't give a shit what people thought. She looked again for a place to sit, but everyone in the class was either scared—or jealous. Samantha might as well have been invisible. I slipped my backpack under my knees, then waved and pointed to the only empty space in the room, on the floor in the corner next to me.

"Thanks," she whispered, as she slid in. "At least there's one human being here."

We went to lunch after, at the Half-Day Café. We had to. We really were the only two normal people in the class.

"Okay," Samantha started, as we walked over, "on a scale of one to ten, maybe, oh, I don't know, negative fourteen?"

"The teacher?"

"I'm never gonna make it. Doesn't she know we're all dummies?"

"I recommend Cliff Notes."

"No kidding."

The next hour flew by. We talked about flunking our senior years, hating how good-looking guys think you're supposed to drool all over them, and Samantha's mother—who sounded almost as bad as mine. I found out she did not like to be called "Sam," that most people called her "Sammie," and that she used to be a dancer. And that—thank God—she did not see the point of going to college, making her the only other person in the entire universe that thought like me. She just wanted to move out and get away from her mom and "all those people I've been in school with forever."

"I can't be myself with them," she explained, between mouthfuls of salad. "You know what I mean? They expect me to be like I was in high school."

"I know *exactly* what you mean." I barely managed to drink my iced coffee, I was so high off talking with her.

"You work at McDonald's, huh?" she asked. "You get to wear one of those cute outfits?"

"Oh yeah, I look really good in it."

"At least you earn your own money."

"Right, minimum wage—big bucks, babe. But I really do it for the customers, you know? They're so . . . *pleasant.*"

"I can imagine."

"Yeah, well, I won't be there much longer. I'm gonna get my stupid diploma and find a job in an office, where I don't have to be nice all the time. I'm taking typing, so I'll . . . oh shit, what time is it?" I glanced at the clock and started gathering my stuff. "Hello . . . typical Mona, late again. See you tomorrow?"

"Wait, what are you doing later today?" she asked. "I mean, do you want to go start that research thing?"

I couldn't quite keep the smile from taking over my entire face. "Okay. Uh, three o'clock?"

I didn't bother to tell Samantha it was my birthday, or anything really personal. I'd learned that in high school. When your mom moves every six months or so, your social life sucks. There are always people to hang out with, especially if you act like you fit in, but they're not really *friends*. The second you have your own opinion about something, it's like you never existed. So I was willing to wait before I tried too hard with Samantha. I figured the less she actually knew about me, the easier it would be when she decided to stay away.

But the next morning, she called my house to see if I wanted a ride to school. We studied together again that afternoon, and she dropped me at Mickey D's for my evening shift. Wednesday, same thing. *And* Thursday and Friday—then we made plans for the weekend. She was the easiest person in the world to talk to, and she liked whatever I said. She didn't seem to mind if I wore my pants baggy or tight, what I did with my hair, or how my house looked. And I couldn't believe how much we laughed! I had to consider that maybe she was different—she didn't need me to be anything but myself. And after only two weeks, it felt like we'd been friends forever.

"Let's get a place," I blurted one night, as we sat outside my house in her Jeep. Term papers were due the next day, and we'd spent the entire evening in the library, finishing them.

"Okay, sure. Want me to write the check, or will you? Oh, I know. I'll put it on my credit card!"

"You can find a job, Clueless, and I'll get a real one," I argued, then smiled. "And maybe your dad'll help out?"

"Wait a minute, how did my dad get into this?"

"He's rich, isn't he?"

"No, he isn't rich."

"Oh. Isn't he the dad that gave you this Jeep? The same one that has a cabin in Aspen?"

"Yeah, well, he still isn't rich. He sort of . . . has money."

"So get him to give some to us."

"What about *your* dad?"

"The one I haven't seen since I was three? Oh yeah, good idea, hand me your cell."

Samantha finally broke down and called her father. Her mom was out with the boyfriend, Bruce, so we had the place to ourselves, and we were both absolutely manic. She walked around with the cordless; I trailed and tried to listen in.

"What about college, honey?" was the first thing he asked.

"Nope. Not right now."

"What does your mother say about that?"

"Like I told her?"

"Sammie . . ."

"Daddy, be real. Why would I tell *her*?"

"Well, because you live there. Because she's your mom."

"Yes, and totally obsessed with me going to college."

"Only because she never got a chance to go."

"That's not my fault."

"No one said—"

"Anyway, she's getting married next summer. And I do *not* want to live with Bruce."

"Your mother's getting married?"

"Yep."

He sighed. "Good for her. Well, honey, Ruthie and I would love to have you, but this place is not set up for—"

"No, no, no. Daddy—you are not hearing me. I want to *get*

a job and *move* out of here, and *find* an apartment with my girl-friend from summer school. Mona Brocato. You'd like her." She got it all out in one breath.

"I don't know, Sammie. Your mother feels—"

"I'm eighteen, Daddy, I can do what I want."

He chuckled a little. "Yes, that's true. But then why are you calling me?"

"Because . . ." She threw a panicked look in my direction. "You know, I just need some . . ." I shoved a paper in front of her and frantically started jotting down notes. She nodded. ". . . advice. We don't have credit or references, or a security deposit . . ."

I scribbled some more and crossed my fingers.

". . . or even know where to find a place we could afford. So I thought maybe you would have some ideas." Samantha crossed her fingers, too, and pressed them up against mine.

"Sounds like I'm being hit up for a loan."

"Anything you can do, Daddy, would really help." We both held our breath.

He chuckled again. "Do you know how proud I am of you?"

"I don't know why." She said it almost under her breath. I wasn't sure he even heard.

"You had a rough year, honey. And you handled it." His voice sounded like a father's for a minute, and Samantha turned slightly away from me.

"It's not like I had a choice."

"I know. But, still. I'm just sorry we couldn't come to the funeral. We wanted to, but . . ."

"No problem, Daddy, it's all right."

"You're a great kid, Sammie. I'm very proud of you."

It seemed an eternity before her dad spoke again. I realized I was still holding my breath.

"Come to think of it, there *is* a guy who owes me a favor. And he *does* happen to own an apartment building you kids might be able to afford. I'll call him tomorrow. *If* he's got a vacancy, and it's reasonable, I'll help you out. Deposit and two months' rent. But then you're on your own."

I let out a silent cheer and started jumping all over the house.

"Omigod, Daddy, are you serious? That would be awesome."

"Well, Baby, it's the least I can do."

When she hung up, we just stood there, staring at each other. She slowly shook her head. "I don't believe I just did that. I haven't talked to my dad in months."

My stomach dropped down around my knees. *Great. Another stupid Mona-move.* I opened my mouth, but nothing came out for a second. Then all I could manage was, "I'm sorry, I thought you . . ."

She half-smiled. "No, no. You don't understand. This is good. Even if he doesn't really do it."

"Okay. I can't say I get what you mean, but . . . okay."

"Mona, you just witnessed a miracle. My father *never* talks to me this long."

Mona

Our house was at the bottom of a hill in Fairfax, at the end of one of the old unpaved county roads. The yard was overgrown with scruffy-looking bushes, and somebody had planted an avocado tree dead center—which did not ever once grow avocados. The house itself was tiny, the paint was peeling, and the crud on the kitchen floor was permanent. Trust me, I tried—no amount of Lysol and scrubbing could get it off. My bedroom only had one little window, which opened practically against the hill. But it was way better than an apartment, where everybody is in your business all the time, and at least we'd managed to stay longer than a few months.

Samantha had never come in, even though she'd been there tons to pick me up or drop me off—mostly because I'd never invited her. I wasn't ashamed, really, just careful. But this time, I didn't have a choice. You can't go running around by yourself at three in the morning, even in Marin County.

It'd started the night before. I'd picked up on the behavior, right off, but I was still in my little fantasy world of moving out with Samantha, and my early warning system wasn't functioning so good.

"Finished summer school?" Mom asked, peeking over my shoulder at the newspaper I was reading. I folded it over slowly, hiding the apartment for rent column.

"Sure did, Mom. Last week." I smiled up at her, feeling that familiar little gnawing in my gut. "Thank goodness, huh?"

"Think you passed this time?" She sat on the other side of the couch, eyes burning into mine.

"Yeah, I think so." I kept my voice light and sincere and smiled even more. Sometimes I wondered how the hell I did it. "I know I did good in typing. I can't wait to stop working at McDonald's."

"Well, you don't always get a choice in life. You remember that."

"I sure will."

She tilted her head just that little tiny bit to the left, narrowed her eyes almost imperceptibly, and paused before asking, "Ramona, are you mocking me?"

This was the test. I had to keep eye contact and find the exact inflection—not flippant, but not over-serious either. "No, Mom. Of course not." And then I had to not say too much. With a little nod, she sat back on the couch and picked up the rest of the paper.

"Better not. You just better not," she said quietly.

That's when I should've made my just-in-case preparations. But I chose to let it pass, and went back to daydreaming about the apartment with my new best friend. My only friend, as a matter of fact, but who was counting. And maybe she wasn't truly a best friend yet, but I was sure she would be. I had a very strong feeling about it.

I circled a couple of ads, completely ignoring the rents. There was no way two teenagers would be able to afford an apartment in San Francisco, but I had a feeling about moving, too. I could see us together, hanging out, cooking dinner, watching whatever we wanted on TV, and going out whenever we wanted to. Samantha's dad had connections—he'd definitely find something.

Mom clanged around in the kitchen for a while and then went to her room. She didn't say good night. If I'd peeked in on my way to bed an hour or so later, I probably would have seen her sitting up in her chair, brewing. Instead, Stupid One forgot that Mom had new meds. Maybe, in my head, I was already out on my own.

At three in the morning, she opened my door, *not* quietly, and planted herself in the doorway. With the hall light on behind her, you could only see her outline, and my mom is a big woman. So when the door banged open, slamming me awake, it was a monster I saw standing there.

"Shit!" It got out before I could stop it.

My mother took a step into my room. *"What did you say?"*

Too late for smiles or careful inflections.

"Are you cussing in my house?" The tone was there. Every word clearly enunciated, the voice flat and low. She was pretty far along.

"Sorry, Mommy."

"And what's *this*?" She held up the newspaper I'd left on the floor by the couch. The one with all the apartments circled.

"Nothing." I shrugged and tried to scan the dark room for my stuff.

"*I* don't think it's nothing. *I* think you better tell me what's going on around here."

My voice stayed remarkably calm. I knew there was not even a bit of expression on my face. "It's really nothing, Mom." If I could get out, I'd go to my Aunt Mollye's. We'd call the doctor, and everything would work out okay. Except Mom had the car keys, and my purse was who-knows-where.

I repeated the litany in my head: *It's not her fault—it's the disease talking. She can't help it, don't take it personal.* It always surprised me how calm I could get. Almost like I could think in hyperspeed and slow down time enough to be able to act. Like playing soccer—she'd move and I'd counter, she'd accuse and I'd have to find a way to answer the accusation without making her feel even more threatened. I managed to pick up a sweatshirt as I talked, and moved a little, and talked, and moved some more. I got us out to the living room.

"I really want to talk about this, Mom, but can you wait just a sec? I have to use the bathroom." She nodded and I bolted, the cordless already stuck up my sleeve. I called my aunt.

"Hello, you've reached Ford and Mollye . . ." Shit, of course they were sleeping. Not a chance they'd hear this before tomorrow. I hung up the phone. Not good. No purse, no keys, no way to get anywhere by myself. I didn't have any other choice. Even though it was 3 A.M., I dialed Samantha.

"'Lo?" a bleary voice answered.

"Can you come get me?" I whispered.

She came instantly awake. "What? Who is this? Mona?"

"Yeah."

"What time is it?"

"I don't know. Can you come? And hurry? Please?"

By the time she got there, a half-hour later, Mom had hit the scary part, where she really wasn't seeing me at all, the part where she fired off accusations so bizarre there was no way to answer them. When I heard the Jeep, I seized the moment, edged toward the door and suddenly sprinted out of the house. Mom was right behind me.

Samantha's mouth actually hung open. Why not? Most of her other friends probably didn't race around outdoors in the middle of the night wearing boxers and a T-shirt. Or have crazy mothers that woke the entire neighborhood with their screaming.

"That your little *whore* friend?" Mom yelled, right on cue, pointing at Samantha. "The one who won't come in the house?"

"Go inside, Mother," I said, not turning around. I threw a dirty look at the couple next door; they'd ventured out for up-close and personal. "What are *you* looking at?"

My mother never even noticed them. "You're not fooling me, you slut. I know what you're doing. You're just like your father, always sneaking around."

Samantha flung the car door open and I was almost safe when my mom swooped into the front yard, and scooped up a handful of gravel. She grunted as she pitched it at us. A couple of sharp stones got me on the thigh and I yelped. The neighbor woman backed away. The man pointed his finger.

"That's it. That's *it*. We're calling the police, you. . ." he said. Samantha did a U-turn and floored it, but the wheels spun in the dirt and then the car died. I started to laugh.

"Oh shit, don't die now . . . oh shit . . . go, please go," I urged, rocking in the seat as if the motion would make a difference. My mom was now screaming at the neighbors. The woman cowered behind her husband, who was screaming back, and they both inched toward their front door. Just then, the ignition caught. We drove a few blocks before Samantha pulled over and turned to me.

"Omigod. What the hell was that?"

I giggled nervously. "Well, um, Samantha, that was my mom," I told her, feeling my cheeks get hot. "I think maybe I pissed her off."

"Yeah." She rolled her eyes and giggled a little, too. "I think maybe you did."

"Yeah, well, thanks for coming." The giggles faded. The last time a friend had witnessed my mother, it'd been all over the school that I lived with a crazy woman.

"No problem." She'd settled, too, and looked at me with concern. "You're sure you're okay?"

"Fine." I couldn't meet her eyes. "Thanks. I mean—"

"Hey, what are friends for, huh?" She started the car again. "Wanna come over?" Then she giggled again. "Of course you do, where else are you gonna go?" She headed out down Sir Francis Drake. It was strange; we had the whole street to ourselves.

"You could drop me at my aunt's, if you want."

"Hey, you woke me up. You're going to keep me company."

"Yeah, but your mom—"

"Is sleeping with Bruce tonight. At his house."

* * *

My shoulders had relaxed by the time we got to Samantha's, in Mill Valley. I loved this house, with the huge willow in the back yard and a view of Mount Tam from the living-room window. As she shoved a frozen pizza into the micro, I changed into some of her sweats. We settled in the kitchen, and all of a sudden, I noticed she wasn't looking me in the eye. This was it, no doubt. End of story. So much for having a friend.

"Sorry about my mom," I said, as I opened the Coke she handed me.

"Will you stop?"

"She's got bipolar disorder."

"Okay. Whatever. It's not a big deal."

But I had to explain. "You heard of manic-depressive?" I went on. She nodded. "Same thing."

"Oh." She set the pizza down and cut us two pieces. "Is it serious?"

"Well, she's on meds now, so it's not so bad as it used to be."

"It used to be worse?"

"Or maybe I'm just used to it." I dropped my head forward and looked up at her through my lashes. "You should see when she goes off at dinner."

"Why? What happens?"

"Never mind—it's way too strange."

"Come on. What? Say it."

"No. You'll make me leave."

"Mona!"

"Okay, okay." I grinned and shrugged a little. "She throws

things. Like, she'll toss a chicken breast or something . . ."

Try as she did to keep a straight face, Samantha started to giggle. "She throws chicken at you?"

"Yeah, or hamburger; whatever's close. Once she did the broccoli, too. Actually, she started with the broccoli, followed with the pork chops and was going for the silverware when I managed to get out of the house."

"Damn."

"Yeah. Then after, she's pissed 'cause the house is dirty. Which is *my* fault because *I* made her do it in the first place. So . . . she throws the cleaning stuff at me."

"You're making this up."

"I wish I was." I ducked my head and "watched" a pretend bottle whiz by. "Whoops! There goes the Lysol!" We both fell out laughing.

"Oh man, my stomach hurts," Samantha gasped, then shook her head. "I'm sorry—it's not really funny, is it?"

"I don't know. It sounds kinda funny to *me*."

"Yeah, but . . . oh shit, that's why you never had me over, huh?"

"Hello! What do you think?"

"Why didn't you just say something?"

"What am I going to say? 'Come to dinner, but if she picks up a chicken breast, run'?"

Mona

"There's a reason we both took that English class, you know," I yelled, as we headed across the overpass toward the freeway. Riding in Samantha's Jeep with the top down and the music blasting was my new favorite thing to do. It felt like flying.

"Because we flunked it the first time?" We slowed for a stop sign, and she maneuvered her hair into a knot and stuck a pencil through it.

I leaned forward to relight the roach I'd been smoking. "Nope. Because we needed to meet each other."

"Put that away, would you?"

"It's karmic. It's very karmic."

"You're very wacked."

"Time will tell, my friend. Time will tell." As we rounded the turn to the freeway, I offered her the pot again. She waved it off and rolled her eyes at me. "Sorry, I forgot." A picture of my mom's screaming face flashed through my head, and just as quickly disappeared. Was that just *this* morning? I loved how, right this moment, I didn't care *at all*. I looked over at Samantha. "How can you *not* like pot?"

* * *

Way up past Santa Rosa, we left the freeway, and all of a sudden, we were in complete country-time, going thirty-five on a two-lane road, past cows grazing and old funky barns and farmhouses. Ancient signs announced the towns, and main streets lasted all of two minutes. Samantha grinned at the way I kept looking around. Finally, we drove over this weird-ass bridge, which looked just like an oversized Erector set. "I thought we were going to a river."

"Right there." She pointed down at a wide stream of greenish water.

"*That* is not a river, Samantha."

"Shut up. That's the Russian River." She made a face at me. "What did you expect?"

"Well, you know, the basics—*water*, preferably a *lot* of it, traveling in one direction."

"It *is* traveling in one direction."

I punched her on the arm and pointed to an empty parking space along the main street, a half-block of little stores and mom-and-pop restaurants. "I can't believe this place, it's a time warp. Where's the Jack in the Box? I'm hungry."

"You just ate." She glanced over. "In fact, I think you ate everything we brought."

"So? I'm hungry again."

We got BLTs to go from Ann Sophie's Home Cooking, and headed toward the shore. I caught a glimpse of us in the window of Gene's Hardware Store and smiled. What a team. Black-haired and blonde, dark-skinned and pale. We could do the cover of *Vogue*. Samantha looked to see why I was smiling, and sucked her breath in, hard.

"What?" I asked. "What is it?" I looked around, trying to see what had startled her.

"Nothing." Her voice was sharp, cutting, a tone I'd never heard before.

"Shit, that wasn't 'nothing.' What happened?"

"It's nothing, okay? Really. I thought I saw someone I knew. No big deal. Come on." Her tone was still harsh. She stepped off the boardwalk and turned a corner, and boom, we were surrounded by naked babies and their fat moms. Something stabbed me in the foot.

"Ow! Shit, shit, shit! This is not a *beach*, Samantha, this is a goddamn rock field." I stopped to dig out the stone that had wedged itself inside my sandal, and tried to ignore the dirty look I was getting from the nearest mom.

"Miss Brocato? Do you complain about *everything*?"

"Hello? Is it too much to ask for a beach you can *walk* on?" I smiled at the mother but she turned away. "Hey, are we *in a riverbed*? Because this is nothing like you promised."

"The water's low this month, okay? Sit down and eat your sandwich."

"I will." I dug in as Samantha slipped off her shoes and leaned back. I could tell from her eyes, she was off somewhere else.

"Hey." I nudged her gently. "Are we still friends?"

"Nope."

"No, I mean it."

She glanced over. "Why are you always asking me this?"

"Just answer. Do you still like me?"

"Why wouldn't I?"

"I don't know. My weird mom. Me smoking."

"Shut up." She started chuckling and shaking her head.

"See? I knew it! You hate me."

"Will you relax?"

"I can't. You're laughing at me."

"No, I'm not, Mona. I'm liking you."

"What?"

"Never mind. Come on. Want to wade out to the float?" She pointed and I could see that one part of the river, the area nearest the hill on the far shore, actually did have water rushing through. In the middle sat a large wooden platform tied to a pole.

"Sure." We both rolled up our pants and ventured into the water. Ten feet out, water lapped gently against our calves. One of the naked babies stood a few yards away with his mom, giggling and holding on to his little dick. "Oh fine. Look, he's peeing," I said. "Some river you brought me to."

"Yeah, well, be careful," she cautioned. "It's deeper out there, and some places, the shore drops off."

"Uh-huh."

"And watch out for the baby tiger sharks." I grabbed her arm and she giggled. "Kidding, I'm kidding."

I took a few steps forward and suddenly, instead of hitting the river bottom, my feet slid out from under me. Bingo—there I was, *under* the water. Samantha was laughing hysterically when I came up. I lunged at her, and she dove in. I dove right behind her.

"Whoopsie," she said, grinning, after we'd both pulled ourselves up on the float. "You fall down."

"You're a shit, you know that? '*Wade* out to the float?'"

"Cooled you off, didn't it?"

"Yeah, but look what happened to my lunch." I pulled the soggy bread and Saran wrap out of my shirt.

"You put the sandwich in your pocket?"

"I told you I was hungry," I answered, taking a bite.

"I cannot believe you're eating that!" She laughed as I munched away. "Stop," she begged. "I'm going to pee my pants."

"Do it in the river like everyone else."

She laughed more. Finally, it petered out, and we relaxed back onto the float. The sun melted into my body, and I drifted off to a half-sleep, where I could still hear the voices from the kids on the shore, but nothing in the world could bother me. An hour or so later, when I drifted back, Samantha was lying on her side, gazing out at the river.

"Hey," I half spoke, half whispered.

"Good sleep?" She glanced over and smiled as I sat up.

"Awesome. You?"

"Nope. Just sat here and watched you make silly faces."

"Great. I'm going to be living with a voyeur."

"Yeah, well, don't count on it, okay? My dad's not big on the follow-through."

"Who cares? We'll get our own."

"Right."

The river gently lapped against the float. "Samantha? What was it that happened to you?"

"When?"

"Last year, I guess? I don't know. Your dad was talking about it."

"Oh." Her eyes changed and she looked away from me. "My best friend died."

I felt like I'd run headfirst into a brick wall. "Shit, Samantha, I'm sorry."

"Why? You didn't do it."

"No, I mean . . . God, I'm sorry."

She shrugged. "It's okay."

Moments of quiet went by and I had no idea what to say. "You must miss her a lot," I blurted. *Good, Mon. That was intelligent.*

"Actually, I don't think about it much."

"What was her name?"

"Jules."

"Jewels? Like diamonds and rubies?"

She smiled. "No. Julie, Juliana, actually. But I called her Jules."

"Oh. Can I ask . . ."

"Cancer."

"Damn. I'm sorry. Was she . . ."

"I really don't like to talk about her. Okay?"

"Sure."

"I mean, it's past. There's nothing I can do. So what's the point, right?"

"Right. I understand. I really do." *Shut up, Mona. Change the damn subject.* "Hey, thanks for coming to get me this morning."

"Sure." She flashed a big smile, stood up, and held a hand out to me. "Okay. So you know about the trick getting back, right?"

"Great. There's a trick?"

"Yep."

"Okay, what do we do?"

"You stand over there, and face out." I did. "Good. Now take a big breath . . ." I did that, too, and the next thing I knew she'd sent me flying into the river. Samantha dove in from the other side, and I chased her back to the beach.

Samantha

Sunlight sneaks around the edge of the curtains, fills the bedroom, and teases me gently from a deep, dreamless sleep. I yawn and stretch and glide up, taking my time, liking how my bare legs slip on the sheets, enjoying the sensation of waking. . . .

Then I remember.

Jules died.

My body stops moving.

The air begins to disappear.

I know it all one more time, every second fresh, like a horrible surprise, brand-new, overwhelming.

The walls of my room slide closer.

I can't hear the birds I see chirping in the front yard.

I can't tell if the pain is inside me or out.

A shadow outlines the sun and slowly starts filling it in.

The sound of Mona softly snoring brought me back. She was curled up like a puppy around my spare pillow, her long hair tossed up behind her, framing her face. Her mouth was slightly open. One arm was hanging over the edge. Suddenly she snorted a little and turned over. I smiled. Even when she was sleeping, she made me laugh.

A little tap at the door, and my mother stuck her head in. "Breakfast?" she chirped.

I held my finger to my lips and pointed at Mona. Mom nodded.

"Okay. When you're ready."

I stuck my tongue out at the door after she shut it. She was watching me again, sneaking, like she did in May, thinking I didn't know. She had the boyfriend, Bruce, doing it, too. Every word I said, every look, got sucked up and analyzed. When I didn't talk, they watched me more, sending secret messages to each other across the room. Even Mona had noticed it. And, just like before, Mom was dropping college pamphlets all over the house. Like that would make a difference? She even dragged my dance bag out of the back of the closet and left it on my bed, with a paid-up dance card tucked in the top. I tossed it back into the closet and ignored her stupid smiling-inquisitor looks.

The worst had been a few afternoons ago when my old dance teacher, Linda, showed up about an hour before Mona and I were supposed to get together. Funny how my mom had asked just that morning about our plans. Linda brought Brooke and Colleen, two of the girls from my dance company, and we all sat in the living room, pretending it was perfectly normal for people I hadn't seen in two months to drop by out of the blue. Of course my mother was in on it. I could tell by the arrogant little smirk she had on her face as she left us alone "to talk." Linda did most of the talking, Colleen couldn't figure out where to look, and Brooke made constant eye contact with me, grinning and nodding. I just waited, wishing Mona was there.

"We're doing the tour, Sammie," Linda finally announced, which was of course the whole reason for the visit and no doubt, my mother knew it. She nodded to Colleen, who managed to actually look at me as she handed me a clipping:

The Fifth Street Dancers, under the direction of choreographer Linda Marcelle, will be traveling to Los Angeles later this year for a week of performances throughout the area. This tour, called THE JULIANA TOUR, was originally scheduled . . .

That's when I left the room. I don't know where I got the guts to do it, but I stood right on up and smiled and said, "I'm really sorry, but I have plans. I have to go get ready." They stood up, too, looking at each other like they couldn't believe what I'd just said. "It was really nice to see you. Good luck with the tour." My mom sashayed in, pretending she hadn't been listening at the door.

"Sammie? What are you doing? You have guests."

"Sorry. I have to pick up Mona. I told you that this morning, remember?" I did the hug-kiss-see-you-soon exit and was on my way to Fairfax. I'm not quite sure how I even got there, I was so pissed. But if Mona noticed anything—which she must have— she left it alone. She launched right into a story about a job interview she'd had, where she pretended she was an expert in this random computer software, and it turned out to be the main one they used.

"You shoulda seen me! I didn't even know how to open the damn program," she said. I couldn't stop laughing. And things slid right back into place.

But of course it wasn't over. Mona spent the night, hung out, and even had dinner with my mom and Bruce. We headed for my room the second we were done, so we could put together a job-hunting plan for the next day. It wasn't going so great, and it was starting to not be very funny. Basically, nobody really cared.

"*Experience?*"

"*Uh . . . none.*"

"*College?*"

"*No, but I did graduate from high school.*"

"*And what do you think you could bring to our company?*"

"*Um, nothing, actually, but I really need a job.*"

Yeah. Right.

"Sammie?" Mom said as I came out a bit later for something to drink. She used that quiet *meaningful* tone, which made Bruce shift slightly in his chair. I paused and looked over at her. "Don't you miss Julie at all?"

A chill shot up my spine, but I managed to keep it from showing in my face. I grabbed a couple of juice boxes and shut the fridge.

"Sammie, I'm talking to you."

"I know."

"Aren't you going to answer?"

"No. It's a stupid question." I started back toward my room, but Mom had had a few glasses of wine, which always made her brave. She followed.

"Hold on a minute, please."

I stopped and stared at her, but didn't speak.

She sighed. "You know, I'm about up to here with you these days."

"Sorry."

"Why were you so rude to Linda and the girls?"

"Why did you ask them over without telling me?"

"They're your friends. I thought you'd enjoy seeing them."

"Well, I didn't. Can we talk about it later? Mona's waiting."

"Life doesn't just stop, Sammie," Mom said. "You have to keep going."

"I do. Every day." My voice came out surprisingly low, like it could only manage the bottom register.

"Then why not be part of the tour? It would be such a good—"

"I don't want to."

"I thought dancing was the most important thing in your life."

"Not anymore."

She glared a second and, for the first time since she'd started smoking again, lit a cigarette in front of me.

"Could you please do that outside? It stinks up the whole house." She didn't listen, just took a huge drag and blew out the smoke.

"You're going to see a therapist. I've already made the

appointment." Without giving me a chance to respond, she stomped back out to the kitchen. I stared down at the floor a second, then followed.

"I'm *not* seeing any therapist, Mother," I told her. "And I don't appreciate you bringing this up right now. I have a guest."

"It's been almost two months, honey."

"So?"

"You're acting like she never existed. You don't even cry."

I opened my mouth, then shut it again. Nothing I could say could possibly explain. "I'm going to take Mona home in a few minutes."

"You can't pretend this didn't happen, Sammie. You need to talk about it. You can't just go and find somebody who looks like her and—"

I couldn't believe I'd heard right. *"What did you say?"*

"Mona. She looks like Julie."

"She does not! Not even a little bit."

"All right, okay, calm down. You still need to face things."

I stared at the pattern in the linoleum, to try to find my center again. "We need to talk some other time."

"You need to deal with this, Sammie."

"Some other time, Mom."

"You're in denial. You're pretending it didn't happen."

"That's really stupid. I know it happened."

"Do you? Do you really?"

Something in the tone of her voice disconnected the brain from the mouth. "Yeah, actually I do. You want me to say it? Why don't I say it—she died. *Jules died.* She's dead. Not living.

Gone. Outa here." I shrugged at her. "See? No denial. How's that? Is that good?"

"Sammie . . ."

"I know because I was there, remember? That was *me* in the hospital with her and her mom . . ."

All the nurses smile, but their faces are closed to me. I know I'm walking toward her room. I just don't know how I'm ever going to get there. Sandra takes my hand and leads me down the corridor and everything inside me is screaming this can't really be happening, but it is, and there's Jules, on the bed . . .

". . . so you just leave me alone, okay? This doesn't belong to you."

"You're going to see a therapist, Sammie. That's all there is to it."

"Maybe *you* should see a therapist. You're the one who's in *denial.*"

"Listen to me—"

"You never even went to see her, Mom—not at the hospital, not at her house, not the whole fucking time she had cancer. So don't talk to me about denial, okay?"

"Sammie, watch your language . . ."

"Sandra would have come to see me." My mom snapped her head away, like she'd been slapped. I started back toward my room and Mona. I did not want Jules in my head right now.

"That's not fair, Sammie," Bruce said, from his post by the

door. He had sneaked in to listen while we were arguing. "Your mother did the best she could."

"My mother did nothing. And neither did you. Or my father, okay? Let's just get all that shit straight."

"It was a difficult situation," Bruce went on.

"It wasn't a 'situation,' Bruce. It wasn't a fucking *situation*." I took a deep breath and concentrated hard and somehow regained a bit of control.

The room grew quiet. Too many memories were out; I didn't know how to sort through them. I didn't know how to be nice. I wanted this all to disappear. Pieces were ripping loose inside me, and Mom looked like she would bust out crying, any second, and never stop. I needed this argument to end; I needed to be back in my room, planning my life *now* with the friend who was alive. I sighed.

"You know what? It doesn't matter. Let's just drop it." She didn't seem to hear. I shrugged again, desperate for a door back to "normal." I lightened my voice. "We'll talk more later, okay?" I tried for a smile. "Mona probably needs to get home." She nodded, once, and I started toward my room.

"Sammie?" she called in a low voice. I turned around but didn't speak. This time we locked eyes. Then the strangest thing happened—all of a sudden I wanted her to hug me, to pull me over and sit me on her lap and stroke my hair, like she used to do when I was a very little girl. I wanted Mom-words to convince me everything would work out and that nothing this bad lasts forever. I wanted to know she'd hold me if I started to fall apart. And—for one incredible second—I thought she would. I could see her, in my mind's eye, reaching for me. . . .

Instead, she dropped her gaze to the floor, and shrugged her shoulders in a helpless, little-girl way. Bruce inched closer and patted her arm. When she looked up at me again, her eyes were veiled.

"Nothing, Sammie. Never mind." She threw me a vacant smile. "Drive safely. I'll leave the lights on."

Samantha

Mona touched my arm as we headed out toward the Jeep. "You okay? Want me to drive?" she asked.

I shook my head and glanced back at the house. Of course my mother was right there, staring out the window.

"I do know how to drive a clutch."

"I'm fine."

We climbed in and I started down the street. Mona leaned the seat back and swung her legs up on the dashboard, scrunching back just like Jules always did.

"So," she announced. "I have a plan. Wanna hear it?" With her long hair hiding her face, for a second, she looked exactly like her.

"Could you not do that?"

"Do what?"

"Your feet. Could you take them down?" I used the nasty tone I should've saved for my mom.

"Sorry," she muttered, dropping her legs and sitting up straight. The silence was claustrophobic.

"No, I'm sorry, Mon. I didn't mean it that way," I muttered, as we headed toward the freeway.

"It's okay."

"It's not, but—"

"I heard your mom, Samantha."

"Oh. Yeah. I guess you did, huh."

"It sucked."

"That's my mom for you." I shook my head a little to clear it, and then tried a smile. "So what's your plan?"

"You know what? It's no big deal."

"No, come on, tell me."

"It's really not important."

"Okay. Whatever."

We got all the way to the freeway exit before she spoke again. "I hate that everybody thinks you're supposed to cry all the time."

"I know."

"I don't cry, and I've got plenty to cry about, you know what I mean? But crying never helps me."

"Me, either."

"It doesn't mean I don't feel anything. I totally feel it."

I glanced over. She was staring at me.

"Like you do," she said softly.

"Yeah."

"Did you cry at all?"

"Only at first. But not at the funeral. And not around school." I snorted, remembering how everybody had moped around, pretending they were Jules's best friend. "Especially not there." I sighed and glanced at Mona. "But I still miss her."

"I know." We pulled up in front of her house. She opened

the door, then paused and met my eyes. "Tomorrow? For the wars?"

I nodded. "See you then."

When Mona walked out her front door the next morning, I had to blink twice to make sure I wasn't hallucinating. This was a girl who liked her mascara. And her eyeliner, and most of the time, her lipstick. But here she was, absolutely clean-faced, with her hair combed straight back into a bun. She was dressed in a skirt and blouse a grandmother would love. When she saw my expression, she laughed.

"It's my plan, okay?" She threw a bag in the backseat. "I'll change to real clothes later. But we are going to San Francisco, and I am Getting This Job."

We got to the financial district in record time. I waited in the downstairs lobby, trying to pretend I belonged with the suits, and ignoring Miss Information Lady as she leaned forward in her booth every two minutes, checking me out. Mona zoomed up sixteen floors to "Campbell & Colburn—An Ad Agency." She was back in fifteen minutes.

"Uh-oh, way too quick," I said as she came out of the elevator. "Told you about those clothes."

"I start a week from next Monday."

"You lie."

She pointed to herself and did a little pirouette. "Hello. Receptionist. Twenty-two thou a year."

There was no way we could get back in the Jeep and drive home, or even *think* about job hunting for me. Mona changed in the lobby bathroom and did her eyes. We hopped the cable car on California and transferred to the one that took you down to Fisherman's Wharf. We sat on the outside, and neither one of us could stop grinning. Every once in a while, we'd look at each other and squeal. The woman sitting next to us moved.

Right past Hayes Street, a whole group of good-looking guys sprinted past, on their way to the next cable car stop. Mona grabbed my arm.

"Shit. I know him," she whispered. I didn't get a chance to comment before the cable car bounced to a stop and they all jumped on.

"Hey, Jason," Mona said, in a surprisingly quiet voice. I took a closer look at her—there was something about this guy that clearly got to her. He gave us an arrogant grin.

"Hey." He looked back at his friends and shrugged a little, like he couldn't quite place her. I felt her body tense. She was pissed.

"Mona. Remember? I was in your English class."

"Oh, right." He made a face at his friends to show he didn't know who the hell she was.

Mona stiffened. "You remember. We were at that party at Amanda's together, and then you and I . . ."

"Yeah, yeah, Mona. 'Course I remember. Whatchu been doing?" He leered at me as he talked.

"Oh, I'm in advertising," she announced, and I barely kept the laughter down. "In Germany." I felt my stomach twitching. "This is my roommate, but she doesn't speak any English. We're here visiting."

"Cool." Jason and his boys checked me out and then he winked. I just smiled. "What's her name?"

"Um, Elka."

"Hey, wassup, Elka?" Jason was practically drooling now. What an asshole. But I smiled back anyway, and launched into this long tirade of very German-sounding words. Mona leaned over and nodded.

"Oh, you're lucky, she likes you," she "translated" to Jason.

"Oh yeah?" He leered again.

I jabbered. Again, Mona "translated." "Uh-huh. She thinks you're cute."

"Yeah, well, tell her she's pretty hot herself."

Now Mona did *her* German imitation. I smiled and winked at Jason. I "talked" some more.

"She wants to know if you have a girlfriend."

"Me? Huh." He threw that macho jerkhead look over at his friends. "No way is *that* gonna happen." They laughed and nodded.

Mona "explained" in gibberish and I gave him my lustiest smile.

"Oh!" Mona told him. "In that case she would very much like to have sex with you today."

I barely contained myself when his face fell. "What? What? I . . . I don't think I got that."

"Sex. You know. She wants to hook up."

"No shit? That's what she said?"

"Yeah, girls are pretty *out there* in Europe."

"Damn." The other guys jostled him a little, with all the finesse of horny twelve-year-olds. I "talked" again, patting the seat beside me.

"Okay, she's ready, come on," Mona told him. "Change places with me."

"Huh?"

"You want it or not?"

"Here?" I grinned, patted the seat next to me and undid my top button. I could feel Mona trying not to love it as Jason looked at his friends for help.

"She's kidding, right?" he stammered.

"I don't think so. People do this all the time in Berlin."

"Oh, well, shit. I mean . . . hey, man, it's cool . . . but I don't play that kinky shit. You know?"

The cable car rolled into the turnaround by Fisherman's Wharf, and we jumped down. I winked at Jason and called to him, in loud, plain English: "Go to hell, asshole!"

"Okay, who was he?" I asked, stabbing a piece of shrimp. We'd finally stopped laughing, and had found an outdoor market for lunch.

"Just a guy from school."

"Uh-huh. And?"

She took a deep breath. "And . . . we hooked up once, at a party. But he didn't know me when we got back to school."

"What a shit."

She shrugged. "My fault. I knew he was an asshole, and I went with him anyway. I've got this thing for good-looking guys."

"Well, you rocked today, Mona. You really did." I took the last shrimp. "'Here, I'll change seats. . . .' Did you see the look on his face?"

"Sure did, you German slut, you." We started giggling again.

We explored the entire wharf and didn't get back to the Jeep until almost six. I kept imagining that this was how it was going to be when we were out on our own. The summer evening sparkled on the water of the Bay and glowed over the hills. We rode in silence for a while.

"Good day, huh?" I said as we crossed the Golden Gate.

"Sure was." She reached over and touched my hand. "*And* I finally have a real job!" I smiled back at her. After a moment, I glanced over and caught her staring at me, a thoughtful look on her face.

"What?" I asked. "I've got something on my chin?"

"Do you think I look like her?"

"Who?"

"Julie. I heard your mom . . ."

"No. Not at all. Just the hair."

"Good." She paused a second. "That *is* good, right?"

"Yeah. That's good."

Samantha

Mona's mom gave her the car—straight out, no strings, so she could get to work.

"It was so strange," Mona explained, as she drove me uptown to get something to eat. "We're sitting around, you know, watching TV, and she's way too quiet and I'm trying to remember if she took her meds, and all of a sudden, she says, 'Mona, I want you to have the car.' Hello! I sit there with my mouth open, and she tells me how much she loves me. 'You're a good girl,' she says. 'You're going to make it just fine.' Then she hands me the keys."

"Damn. Just like that?"

"Yep."

"She didn't even throw them at you?"

"Stop that."

"I thought she was pissed you got the job."

"Obviously not. I get to keep the car when you and I move out."

"*If* we move out," I said.

"*When*, Samantha. The word is when." She looked so intense, I held up my hand to ward her off. She shook her head and swung into the parking lot behind the Depot. "You're such a shithead."

"Yeah, well, if I'm a shithead, *you're* an asshole," I said with a smile. "What a pair, huh?" I looked toward the café and tried to sink into my seat. "Oh damn. Don't park."

"I thought you were hungry."

"Not anymore. Drive, okay?"

"Okay." She backed out and headed toward the drive-through, just as Brooke, Sarah, and Colleen sat down at a table. Dressed in rehearsal clothes, hair pulled back ballet-style, they'd tied their sweatshirts around their waists to cover their butts. It reminded me of how I used to look most of the time. Colleen happened to glance over and saw me, then grabbed Brooke. They all stood.

"Samantha?" Mona said. "Those anorexic girls over there? They're waving at you."

"Keep going," I directed. "Pretend you don't see them."

"Too late." We got caught behind another car pulling out, and they came running up. I made myself smile. Then I noticed they were all staring at Mona.

"Oh my God," Colleen said, holding one hand up to her heart and using the other to grab onto Sarah. "For a minute, I thought . . ."

"Shit, no kidding," Brooke added, with a meaningful glance over at Colleen. "That really freaked me out." Sarah just froze, in a sort of half smile, like she was afraid to say anything.

"It's just the hair," Mona said. "I don't really look like her."

"You do! Even before I saw Sammie in the car, I—" Colleen babbled on.

"So, guys," I interrupted, "how are you?"

Brooke tipped her head to one side. "Well, mad at you, that's for sure. Not doing the tour. Plus, you never called me back." I was reminded of those first days after, back at school, when the three of them tailed me everywhere, wanting to make sure I was "okay."

"Sorry. I've been busy."

"No, it's cool." She smiled her cute smile. "I was kidding. I just wanted to make sure you're coming."

"I don't know, Brooke. I don't think so."

"Sammie!" Colleen jumped in. "We can't have it without you! Right?" She glanced at Sarah, who finally managed to move.

"Right," Sarah said.

"Have what?" Mona asked.

Brooke turned to her. "Well, see, every year since, oh, I don't know, forever, I've had this humongous party in May . . ."

". . . which is a 'thank-God-it's-almost-summer party,'" Colleen explained.

". . . and *everybody* comes . . ." Sarah piped in. I sighed. They had their routine going full tilt now.

". . . the entire class. Every year." Here, Brooke managed to change her expression, like a newscaster does. "But this year I couldn't, you know, because, well, you can't exactly have a party when, you know . . ."

"Jules died in May," I explained, and sat back in the seat, wishing I could get up and leave, the way I did when they'd come over with Linda.

"But life goes on, right?" Brooke said, still looking at Mona, but observing me out of the corner of her eye. I stuffed the impulse to reach out and smack her. "Anyway, I can't just skip it, can I? I mean, it's our last year together."

"You *have* to come, Sammie," Colleen whined. "Please?"

"You can come, too!" Brooke announced to Mona, as if that would make any difference. I sighed. The words in my mouth were so nasty I could practically taste them. Mona touched my arm.

"Omigod, you are so sweet! You *know* we'd love to, but we just can't," she said, in a Barbie-doll voice. "We're moving, did Samantha tell you? To the city. We are *so* busy. We barely have time for our boyfriends. Besides, you know she works now, right?"

"You do?" Colleen asked.

"Yeah," Mona answered for me, sounding more and more like them with every word. I bit my lip to keep from giggling. "Elka Advertising. I'm sure you've heard of it." She grinned and tilted her head just like Brooke, then glanced at her watch. "Oh dear, Samantha. We are so late, and we still have to change." She threw them her Mona smile. "College guys," she explained, turning on the ignition. "You know how they are. Wow, it was really nice meeting you. I've heard *so* much! Sorry we have to run. Bye!" She put her car in gear, and we left them in the parking lot, gaping.

"Oh—my—God," I said, the laughter bursting out of me as we rounded the corner by the Sequoia Theater. "Where the hell did *that* come from?"

"Good, huh?"

"Girl, you are amazing."

"Yeah?" She threw me a smile. "Cool. But hello. I totally can't see you hanging out with them."

"I don't. I hang out with you."

"No wonder. Were they always like that?"

"I don't know. I never really paid much attention."

"Because you had Julie, right?"

"Yep." I swallowed, hard, and leaned back in my seat. Mona noticed. Of course.

"Let's eat at your house, okay?" she suggested, changing the subject. I nodded, but when we rounded the corner to my street, I sat back up.

"Shit. Shit, shit, shit. This is not my day. Look," I told her, pointing at the burgundy Lexus parked in my driveway.

"Bruce got a new car, too?"

"It's my dad, Mona."

"We can bail," she offered. "There's food at my house."

"Yeah, good idea. No. Maybe we should go in? Shit . . . I don't know."

Mona slowed her car down and thought a minute. "Okay, then. Let's just go see what's up. I mean, maybe he found a place."

"I hope not."

"Hello? Did I hear you correctly?"

"Mona, I haven't told my mom."

Mona blinked, then started to laugh. "You're right. It's not your day." She parked in front of my house. "Come on. I'm right behind you."

Of course, Bruce was there, too, making it all completely bizarre. They stood up as we entered, smiling like we'd caught them doing something dirty. Dad had on his business smile,

Mom was smoking, and Bruce looked like a cat trapped in a small room with two big dogs.

Mona touched my back lightly.

"Hey, Daddy," I said, in a voice sounding remarkably easy.

"Hi, babe." He smiled and came over to kiss me, then looked over at Mona. "You must be Mona."

My dad is tall and blond and very good-looking, and I could tell she was totally charmed. She held out her hand, staring at him like he was a movie star or something. "Pleased to meet you, Mr. Russell."

"Call me Vince, please." Mona actually blushed.

"Sammie, your father called about an apartment he found for you," my mom announced, sitting back down. "Funny. I had no idea you were looking." Her voice was icy.

"Omigod—you found us an apartment?" Mona squealed. With my eyes, I warned her to be calm. She shut her mouth and swallowed whatever she was about to say. We sat quietly together on the edge of our chairs.

"As a matter of fact, I did." He threw a small look of triumph at my mom, then turned to me. "However, it appears there's a problem."

"I'll say," Mom jumped in. "What about college?"

"Maybe later, Mom. Not right now. I need some time off."

She shook her head. "Things don't always happen the way you think they will, Sammie."

"Yeah, well, don't worry. *I'm* not gonna get pregnant." I blurted it out, and Mona's knee pressed gently against mine. I sighed. She pushed a tiny bit harder. "Sorry. It's just that right now, I want to be on my own." *And away from you and Bruce and Brooke and Linda and everybody else.*

"You don't even have jobs!" Mom was losing it. "How do you expect to support yourselves?"

"Actually, I do have one," Mona said. "I start Monday."

"And I'm looking," I added.

"I promised the girls I'd help," my dad said.

"Of course you did," Mom snapped.

"Well, Jackie, I happen to think it's the right thing for her to do."

My mom stood up and went for a new pack of cigarettes. She took one out, tapped it hard against the table and then turned back to us. "Well, I don't care. I'm not going to allow it. I have custody. I can say."

"I'm eighteen, Mom. I'm legal." I kept my voice noncon-frontational, but I said it. For a second we all sat there. Mom lit her cigarette, took a drag, and blew out the smoke. Bruce tried to disappear by staring at the floor. Dad leaned back on the sofa.

"Did your father tell you to say that?"

"No."

She turned her glare to him. "You shit, you're loving every minute of this."

My father spoke as if he were addressing a child. "You're the one who asked me over, Jackie. Try to act like a grownup."

"Don't use that tone with me."

He assumed an injured expression. "Look. Sammie called me. I did not approach her."

"Then you should have told me about it. That's the *grownup* way to act."

"As usual, you're overreacting. Sammie's old enough to be on her own. You've got to let go."

"Don't you *dare* tell me how to raise my daughter."

"She's my daughter, too, Jackie."

"You'd never know it, as much time as you spend with her."

"I better get going." My father stood, smiled, and held out his hand to Mona. "I'll be seeing you, I'm sure." I stood and he put his hands on my face and kissed my forehead. "Call me and I'll give you the details." Without even a nod at Bruce, he went out the door. My mom stomped to her bedroom and after a few seconds and a lame smile at us, Bruce followed.

Déjà vu hit, hard, spiraling me back eight years to the day they'd told me they were separating. It had felt exactly like this. She'd been tight, angry, out of control; he'd smiled and talked in the same obnoxiously rational voice. All of a sudden, they'd become two people I didn't know. And I didn't like either one of them.

"You know what?" Mona said, drawing me back to the present. "I don't think I'll ever get married."

Mona

South of Market. The Mission District. SoMa. Sort of a used-to-be-ghetto-now-wants-to-be-artsy kind of neighborhood. Lots of students who had just moved in and families who had been here for decades—in a hodgepodge of apartment buildings and restored Victorians squished up next to industrial warehouses. A big population of floating homeless people, a gang element obvious in the tagging on the buildings and street signs, and children playing foursquare on the sidewalk. Very typical San Francisco.

"There!" I pointed, reading the numbers along the side of the street. "Park . . . park . . . park!" The building was five stories high and had recently been repainted—rather haphazardly —a light lemon yellow.

"It's certainly bright," Samantha said.

"Hello? Do we *care*? *Do we really even care?*" This was fairytale-come-true time. I couldn't stop grinning.

Samantha got out of the car and checked out the neighborhood. "I'm definitely not having my mom over."

"Good choice."

We went up the five steps to our front porch and Samantha pointed to the third button down.

"Omigod!" I gushed. BROCATO AND RUSSELL had been engraved in silver on a classy black background and glued on top of our name slot.

"Had to be Daddy," Samantha said, as she slid her key into the lock. We grabbed each other's hands and walked in.

The first thing was the lobby carpet. Probably put here in the forties and well used—nothing was gonna get this sucker clean. Dark wood panel walls, a dead plant in the corner, and to get to the elevator you had to open a door, then a grate. Luckily it was out of order; I wouldn't have trusted it. The only light was a naked bulb hanging in the center. I kept waiting for Humphrey Bogart to come lurking out of the gloom. The stairs were behind an unmarked door; we made sure to look up the stairwell first, then we sprinted. Second floor, just to the right— apartment 204. Home.

The living room was dingy beige and very small, but it had a window that bowed out over the front street with a brocade window seat right below it. The breakfast nook, just made for the two of us, was part of a kitchen even tinier than the one in my mom's house. There was a long hallway with a bathroom at the end. Our bedroom doors faced each other. One had a bigger window, but the other had its own working sink. I took the one with the sink. Then we tried out the window seat and walked around the place at least nine hundred times.

"Okay, so your dad was right. It does need paint," I said, "but, basically, it's—"

"Perfect?" Samantha finished.

* * *

"Hello. Over there. Omigod," I said as Samantha was parking the Jeep. It was the Saturday before we moved in, and we had to finish the paint. I pointed up the block. Two guys, on line in front of the little coffee shop. Two *incredible*-looking guys. The white guy was just a bit taller, with short, dark reddish-brown hair, and just possibly, I couldn't quite see—blue eyes. The black guy was kind of light-skinned and light-eyed, with dreads hanging halfway down his back. They stood there, like a pair of awesome Greek statues.

"Please let them be our neighbors."

"Don't stare," Samantha warned.

"I will," I told her.

"Come on. We've got work to do."

I grabbed my share of the supplies and trailed her up the stairs to our building. But when I glanced back, the black guy lifted his hand in our direction, and the white guy turned and nodded. I smiled to myself and went inside. Fifteen minutes later, our doorbell sounded.

"Who the hell is that?" Samantha asked, already in her overalls, hair pulled back in a braid, touching up the trim around the front window. "Did you invite somebody over?"

I glanced down. "It's those guys!" I went to hit the buzzer to let them in.

"*What are you doing?*"

"Hello. Opening the door."

"Mona! Are you crazy?"

"Come on, they could be neighbors."

"They could also be serial killers."

"Right. And they somehow knew we were moving in, so they hurried over."

"Hey!" A voice yelled from below. "Hey, Brocato and Russell, we brought you coffee!"

We both peeked out the window, and the white guy held up a tray of cups.

"Serial killers usually don't bring you coffee," I whispered to Samantha.

"Like you know."

"I'm letting them come up."

"Fine. But keep the door open."

They were even cuter up close, and stood politely outside the apartment as we talked.

"I'm Noah," said the white guy, who was so beautiful I could barely catch my breath. "This is Ryan."

"Hi. I'm Mona. This is Samantha. Or Sammie. Whatever." Shit. I never talked right around new guys. Samantha didn't seem flustered at all.

Ryan smiled and indicated the coffee Noah was holding. "We figured you might need some of this."

"We've seen you here all week, but . . ." Noah started.

" . . . you don't drop by girls' apartments after dark, when you don't know them," Ryan finished. "They tend to call the police."

Samantha smiled. "Well, thanks for the coffee, that was really sweet." She gestured and took a step back. "Um . . . want to come in?"

"Sure," Noah said, glancing at his watch and over at Ryan. "We can, for a minute." He handed us our coffee.

"Nice place," Ryan said. "I like the colors."

"Thanks," I managed. *Speak, Mona. Don't be a child.*

"So what do you do?" Noah asked. "Are you lawyers? Students? Actresses? Dog trainers? What?"

"Just a couple of girls painting," Samantha answered. "What do *you* do?"

Ryan smiled. "I'm a student. USF."

Noah pointed at him. "Classical pianist, actually. Probably off to Juilliard next year."

"Wow," I managed.

"UC dropout, currently UN-employed," Noah offered, pointing at himself.

"Well, you could help us paint," I said, and Samantha murdered me with her eyes. Ryan caught the exchange, smiled, and shook his head no.

"Thanks, but Gorgeous here has an interview," he explained. "We're hoping he'll get the gig, we're tired of supporting him."

"Yeah, we better go."

"Well, thanks for the coffee," I told them and held open the door. "See you around?"

"Sure do hope so," Noah answered, grinning. Ryan pushed him gently out, winked at me, and closed the door behind them.

I stood frozen, waiting for my heart to slow down. Samantha went right back to painting. "Well? What do you think?"

"I think I have to go to the bathroom, and we don't have any paper."

"About the *boys*, ditz."

"They're boys. So what?"

Without another word, I stroked her arm with my paint-brush. She looked down at the stripe I'd painted and then up at me, incredulous. "What the hell did you do that for?"

"I felt like it."

She leaned over and painted my cheek. "Me, too." I got the back of her neck, she got my ponytail, and the war was on. In minutes, we were done, out of paint, laughing hysterically in the middle of our floor.

Samantha

Having a key to somewhere your mother can't go is a most amazing feeling. I couldn't keep from grinning as I crammed the last of my stuff into the back of the Jeep. I took one more look at my room, mostly to make sure I had everything I wanted, then put my house key on the counter and quietly closed the door. Tonight was it. Mom, of course, was conveniently out to dinner. But who cared? In about an hour, Mona would be picking up Chinese, and we'd rendezvous in the city to celebrate our first night in our new home. I could hardly wait. There was just one more place I had to go, one more little thing to do—then I'd be done with Mill Valley.

It occurred to me I could probably drive to Jules's blindfolded. I parked, sighed, and sat there for a minute, soaking up the quiet of the neighborhood, probably one of the oldest in the whole town. I loved the ancient redwoods and the sunlight streaming through painted patterns along the street. Mostly, I loved her house, long and low and comfortable, the perfect shade of forest green, a place where no one had ever cared if things got messy. The oak tree in the backyard had a hammock, the ideal spot for two little girls to cuddle and whisper secrets.

Buried under the window by the back bathroom were Harold the turtle, Gizmo the fish, and Velvet, my hamster.

Tonight, Jules's bedroom window was open, and her light blue curtains fluttered through, reminding me of a dancer's arm in arabesque. Sandra's station wagon was parked in the driveway. Jules's pint-sized van sat right next to it, cleaner than it ever used to be.

Suddenly, I remembered my last visit here, after the funeral, over three months ago. Three months! How could that be? My heart started to thud and my hand moved to turn on the ignition. This was no place for me—I was on my way to my new apartment, I'd already said good-bye to my mom. Mona was expecting me by seven.

But you promised you'd visit. Sandra needs to know where you are. She's your other mom. That got me out of the Jeep and up to the front door. The speckled ficus tree Jules and I had planted two summers ago greeted me from the corner of the porch, taller now, its branches tangled and twisted in no special pattern. I knocked, lightly, telling myself if nobody answered right away, I'd leave. But the lock clicked and Sandra opened the door, just a crack. Her face paled and I thought she shook her head, just slightly, as if she didn't believe it was me. I almost took a step backward, but she swung the door wide, reached out her arms, and gathered me in. We didn't talk—just stood together, holding on. Her hand on my back was steady and sure, wonderfully familiar. For a tiny second, we were breathing with the same body; and for that same tiny second, everything was all right.

"Oh, Sammie," she whispered into my neck. "I've missed you."

"Me, too."

Smiling softly, she closed the door, and arm in arm, we headed toward the kitchen. From walls, tables, and shelves, Jules smiled down at me. All the pictures Sandra had put out for the gathering after the funeral were still up, and one in particular jumped out. We were eleven, sitting on the steps of the Belrose, proudly holding up our brand-new toe shoes and grinning maniacally. We were waiting for our very first toe class. I smiled to myself. After the first ten minutes, I'd been ready to give the damn things back. But not Jules.

"I did it, Sam," she'd whispered in the car on the way home, showing me a row of tiny stains on her tights. "I danced till I bled. Like Pavlova."

"Mint?" Sandra asked, drawing me into the kitchen. When I nodded, she turned on the water for tea and I slipped into "my" chair in the corner, feeling under the edge of the table. Jules and I had long ago carved our entwining "S & J" there, in the middle of the night, with her father's Swiss army knife. The water boiled quickly and Sandra brought me a cup. Hers was already on the table—the funny little green one Jules had made in ceramics in ninth grade. She sat down, reached over, and smoothed back a lock of my hair.

"You look nice, Sammie. Pretty as always."

"Thanks."

"I can't believe you're here."

"Yeah, me either." I felt the words about Mona and the apartment circling my brain, but I couldn't quite get them to come out of my mouth.

"How was graduation?" she asked.

"Oh, well, I didn't actually graduate, but I went to the ceremony." I thought of how the principal had called out Jules's name and then asked for a moment of silence, but I didn't mention it. "My mom made me."

A shadow crossed her face, but she kept smiling. "And why didn't you graduate?"

"English. I sort of flunked it."

"Sammie! You're good in English."

"Well, I guess I was rude to the teacher."

"Oh, I see." She got that familiar mom-look on her face and I felt my shoulders relax. "They're flunking for rudeness these days?"

I smiled. "Maybe I didn't actually finish the three final papers."

Sandra smiled back. "Yeah, English teachers are funny that way. They sort of like you to do the work." She took the tea bag out of her green cup and started stirring her tea. I noticed she'd gotten thin. And her face seemed much older.

"It wasn't because I didn't want to. I just . . ."

"I know, Sammie. I know." She lifted the cup with both hands, cradling it, and sighed. "One day at a time, huh? That's what everyone keeps saying."

"Yep."

"So. How's your mom?"

"Okay, I guess. She's getting married."

"Same guy? Bruce? Was that his name? The one that looked like that character from *Saturday Night Live*?"

"That's him. Except he's stopped combing his hair over the bald spot." We chuckled together.

"Well, it'll be good for her. And are you dancing?"

"No. I, uh . . . I don't think I . . . No, I'm not." Then the Mona words bumped into each other and spilled out. "Actually, I got an apart—"

"Shhh, shhh. Just a second." She held up a finger, then stood and cocked her head in the direction of the bedrooms. "I'm sorry. I thought I heard Rosie." She moved to check the tea-kettle, then started to rearrange the utensils hanging on the wall next to the stove. "What were you saying?"

"Um, nothing. It's not important. So, how is Rosie?"

Sandra sighed and when she turned around, her eyes had changed, like she wasn't quite with me anymore. "Well, she has bad dreams a lot, but otherwise she's fine." Putting her hand back on the kettle, she smiled. "How about some tea?"

I glanced at my cup, still half full.

"Right. You have some. Sorry." She sat back down at the table. "Oh, I forgot—we got you a birthday present. Julie did, was it March? Anyway, right after that last chemo." Her smile seemed to freeze into place. "I'm not sure exactly where it is right now. I'll have to find it."

"It's okay."

"Did you do anything special? Eighteen's a big one."

"No. I don't think so. Actually, I don't remember."

"Well, that sounds fine, Sammie. Just fine." She said, obviously not hearing me. We both just kept smiling.

"Sandra? Who are you talking to?" William walked in from the den. I almost didn't recognize him. He had dark circles under his eyes and his skin was pale. His hair hadn't been combed and he had stubble all over his chin. The minute he saw me, his lips drew together and his forehead crumpled and he started blinking to hold back tears.

Sandra's face hardened. He held out his arms and, with one quick glance at her, I went to him. He wrapped his arms around me and started crying, silently, his shoulders and chest heaving, his unshaved cheek scratching the side of my face. I didn't know what to do, so I patted his back.

"Oh, Sammie, Sammie. How did this happen? What are we going to do without her?"

"William." Sandra's voice had a warning tone. "Stop it. Please."

I felt him take a huge long breath. "Sorry." He released me and wiped his face with his hands. "I'm sorry, Sammie. I—"

"Come sit with us if you want," Sandra interrupted, "but please get yourself under control." I'd never heard her voice sound so mean. He didn't answer, just patted my arm and left the kitchen. I glanced at Sandra and sat back down.

"I'm sorry, Sammie," Sandra said.

"It's okay."

"No. It's not. It's not okay at all. It won't ever be. Not ever." I stared, not knowing if she was talking to me or to herself. She didn't seem like Sandra anymore. And he wasn't William. I stood up. There was no way I could mention moving out.

"Well, I better go."

She stood, too. "Yes. Thanks for coming by." She walked me to the foyer. I wanted her to hug me again, but I couldn't ask. I just stood there, this stupid needy smile plastered on my face.

Then William started crying again, and we both looked toward the den. He sat hunched up on the couch, his shoulders moving ever so slightly up and down, his face in his hands.

Sandra's face stiffened into an expression I'd never seen before. Her voice was dull, but harsh. "Good night, Sammie."

I nodded and she opened the door for me. I started to thank her, but she closed the door and turned off the porch light.

She always used to watch me all the way out to my car.

I glanced at my watch—Mona was expecting me in a half-hour—but I just stood there, staring at Jules's car, suddenly not remembering how to move. Then I heard their voices.

"What the hell did you think you were doing?" Sandra demanded.

"Leave me alone."

"Why? Why do *you* get to be left alone?"

"You have to give me time, Sandra. Jesus Christ!"

"You're not being fair, William. Not to Rosie. Not to me."

"It's only been a few months."

"You think I don't know that?"

"Sandra—please, she was my babygirl!"

"She's my babygirl, too, or doesn't that count?"

"Please, can we stop this?"

"I don't get to put *my* life on hold."

"I'm trying. I'll get it together, I promise."

"And what the fuck am I supposed to do in the meantime?"

"Mommy? Daddy?" Rosie's voice. And then silence.

I backed off the porch, sprinted to my Jeep, and crawled inside. Pictures of the past nine years filled my brain: Sandra and William and Rosie and Jules—and me, always me, like a part of the family. Sandra even filled in for my mom several times, at school events or performances. I was with them for dinners, movies, picnics, quiet TV nights, long talks, and adventures.

Like when we were ten, before Rosie was even born, and they took me on their vacation out at Stinson Beach. The first day there, I got caught in the breakers. I kept hitting the ocean floor, my eyes stung with salt water, I had sand in my mouth, I couldn't tell which way was up. I remember thinking it was true how you saw stars when you were just about to pass out, and then there was Sandra's hand to grab me and lift me up to the air. There was William to carry me back to shore. And Jules to hug me when I got there.

But everything had broken. This was a twilight zone now— the house, their faces, especially Jules's car, waiting patiently in the driveway. I didn't belong; it was stupid to think I did. Jules was gone. So was my place in this family. Slowly, I pulled away from the curb. I didn't look back. I thought of Mona. I made a left and then another and headed for the freeway to San Francisco.

Part
TWO

~

"Running away, get to it . . .
Where did you have in mind?"

Samantha

There she was, the same time as yesterday. I switched off my light and slid over to one side so I could peek out of my bedroom window without being noticed. As always, I felt guilty. I had no business spying on this old homeless lady, watching her do what she so obviously didn't want people to see. But I couldn't seem to help myself, and since she didn't know I was there, what was the harm?

I'd noticed her when we'd first moved into our new apartment, and somehow I found myself by the window around this time every night since. I wasn't sleeping much anyway; it was good to have something to do. And she'd only missed twice in the past three weeks.

She moved as if she'd choreographed a dance. First, she rolled her two carts up near the garbage cans by the side of our building. She parked, walked around the carts twice, clockwise, then checked behind her and down the street. If all was clear, she nodded, smiled, and then patted the taller can with both hands, three times on top and once on the front. One more look around. Finally, she delicately lifted the lid and peered in, as if she were at a party examining the hors d'oeuvres. When she found some morsel that appealed to her, she plucked it out, carefully wrapped it in the paper napkins bundled into her front pocket, and tucked the whole thing inside her coat. Then she started from the top and did the whole little dance again—walk, nod, pat, choose, and wrap. It was fascinating. As I watched, I made up stories about her, trying out reasons that might have brought her here.

After her second round, I shifted in my seat and my elbow knocked over the candle on the sill, which hit the window with a dull little thud. Startled, the woman looked up. The streetlight caught her full on, wiping away the wrinkles and showing me a glimpse of what she'd looked like when she was young. I froze, hoping she couldn't see me, but we locked eyes and for the next few seconds, neither one of us could move. Her entire expression changed. "How could you?" she seemed to be saying. "This is mine and you took it." She grabbed both carts and trundled on down the road. And suddenly, I felt lonely, lonelier even than usual. Because I knew she probably wouldn't be coming by again.

I settled back on my bed and waited for sleep. I worried for her, hoping she'd be all right. I worried for me, too. So much in this big old world could go wrong. Dying was no longer something that always happened to someone you didn't really know. The clock said one-fifteen A.M.

"Anybody here?" Mona wailed as she came through the front door—an entire half-hour early. I quietly closed the bathroom door.

"In here," I called, as she stomped into her room, muttering the entire time.

"I hate this stupid job! *Everybody* gets to boss me around, even the guy who delivers packages!" She punctuated the words, first with the clunk of shoes flying into the wall, then the slam of the closet door. I could just see her tearing off her work clothes. "Nobody cares that I'm tired and pissy because I stayed up half the night with my roommate, who, by the way, is *home sleeping*; nobody *cares* about that!" She poked her head into the hallway. "Why are you taking so long? I need you."

"Relax, woman."

"Hello? Do you *know* where I've been all day? With Mrs. Fucking Kiff. Who, by the way, now thinks she's my mother. Samantha, she told me to get a tighter bra!"

"She did not!"

"'You tend to jiggle, Miss Brocato.'" Mona pitched her voice to sound like Mrs. Kiff. "*And* a girdle. 'There are older men in this office, Miss Brocato.' Like I don't notice the perverts? Like they don't stare at my boobs and ask me to lunch? 'Consider some *control*,' she says to me. Believe me, I am *not* the one who needs the control!" She sighed, loudly, and rapped on the bathroom door. "Hello? Would you please come out and talk to me?"

"One minute, okay?" I stared at the mirror. This was it. Now. Or not at all. I knew I couldn't get up my courage twice, and it had taken me all afternoon to get this far. Steeling myself, I grabbed the long braid I'd made of my hair and with my right hand, picked up Mona's sewing scissors. They were every bit as sharp as she'd warned, but I still had to saw back and forth. The sound made tingles up my spine, and then suddenly it was done. I was holding my braid in my hand. What was left on my head didn't even touch my shoulders.

"Okay. Fine." She sat down outside the door. "So how was *your* day?"

"Is that sarcasm I'm hearing?" There was no turning back now. Besides, the hardest part was done. I had a vision—I just had to shape it. I isolated a section of hair and snipped it down to about an inch long.

"Oh no, I love that you get to hang out here all day while I waste my life slaving in an office. At least at McDonald's, I got free food."

"Hey," I teased, "you're the one who had to move out *right now*."

"Yeah, well, I didn't know I was going to have to support you."

"Uh-huh, and whose father paid this month's rent?" *Snipsnipsnip!* This was getting easier. I measured the next section of hair by the one I'd already cut. And I did not watch it fall to the floor. I started feeling almost giddy.

"Okay, okay. But aren't you ever going to find a job?"

"As a matter of fact, Miss *Pleasant* One, I had an interview today at a restaurant down in North Beach. Very trendy and very exclusive. It's called Malone's. And I really want to work there."

"So you got a job?"

"No. Not exactly. Not yet." This was going good now. "I did, however, get majorly cruised by Grumpy of the Seven Dwarfs. Whose name is Sal and who happens to own the place. Who said he'd love to hire me except I look like Alice in Wonderland and maybe I could come back and try again when I grew up."

"Okay, one more time. You did or you did not get this job?" But before I could answer, the downstairs bell rang and Mona scampered off to look. "It's Noah, with Ryan and his girlfriend," she yelled back. "Omigod, what's her name? Oh yeah, Erica. You better hurry up, they have two friends with them. Awesome, amazing, hunk-type friends." I heard her slamming the drawers in her room. "Shit, where's my damn bra?"

Vaguely, I was aware of her buzzing them up. But I didn't really care right then, because all of a sudden I couldn't quite catch my breath. There was a total stranger staring at me from the mirror, a stranger with short hair. Voices floated in from the living room.

"This is Andy," Noah was saying. "He's the intellectual one."

"Hey," said a low voice.

"And Daniel. He's the schmuck."

"Thank you very much," another voice said.

"We brought beer," Ryan announced. "Pop top, you don't even need an opener."

"And—we came to invite you to our party," Andy said. "In honor of our good friend here, Mr. Noah Soon-to-Be-Famous-Model, and his upcoming Gap billboard."

"Are you serious?" Mona asked. "You're a model?"

"Be real, woman," Erica said sarcastically. "What else could he do?"

I glanced in the mirror sideways, and their conversation slipped away. What used to be two feet of hair was now an inch long. *Just breathe*, I told myself. *Breathing is good and this will pass. Hair grows.* I picked up the scissors again and trimmed a little here and there, then used the hand mirror to check out the back. I kept trimming, seeing exactly what needed to be done and doing it as if this short blonde hair belonged to someone else. I showered. I dried off. I picked up the braid and thought of the thousands of times I'd swept it up to a bun for dance class, then shook my head and dropped it into the trash.

Mona's mousse was next. I squirted it in my hand, rubbed it in, and spiked my hair. Finally, I did my eyes—big dramatic stage eyes—and outlined my lips. I tried smiling at my reflection. It was forced at first, but then it came for real.

She didn't look at all like me, this girl in the mirror. She was awesome. No—*fucking* awesome. Her cheekbones stuck out, her eyes were huge, and she could have been on the front of some fashion magazine. I laughed out loud as I imagined Sal's expression when I went walking back into Malone's. I'd wear my tight black jeans and that blue spandex T-shirt, with my Wonder Bra, if I could find it. . . . Mona's knock on the door startled me.

"Hey, are you okay in there?" she asked.

"Just fine. I'll be right out." I started cleaning up the mess.

"Erica and the boys are gone, but Samantha, I am in love. With all of them. Of course, Ryan has Erica and I think Noah likes you, and Andy's not really my type, so oh well—I guess that leaves Daniel. . . . Omigod, you should see him. And guess what, we are going to their party in two weeks, and—"

I opened the door and Mona's mouth dropped open, literally.

"Hello? Who are you? And what did you do with Samantha?"

Mona

"Jealousy's a bitch, isn't it?" Erica asked, with a little chuckle. It was her turn to drive. Since we'd discovered that we worked within blocks of each other, we carpooled and shared the monthly parking fees. Damn good thing, too, or most of the time I'd probably be late. Whoa, good idea, then I could get fired.

Anyway, it made everything easier, having someone to talk to in the mornings. I sure as hell never saw Samantha. It was two weeks now since she'd cut her hair and got the job at Malone's, and the proverbial shit had hit the fan. Her hours had changed, and the one thing I looked forward to all day—spending the evening with her—was now gone. I scowled at Erica.

"I am not jealous."

"What do you call it then?"

"I'm concerned, okay?"

"Mm-hm."

"Why would I be jealous of Samantha?"

"Because she likes her job, and you don't. And she's making new friends there, and she talks about them all the time, and she doesn't hang out with you every night anymore, and Noah wants to jump in her pants, and you wish Daniel wanted to get in yours, and—"

"All right, all right. But I am not jealous. I'm worried, okay?"

"Well, that's silly. She's doing good." Erica hit the horn and brakes at the same time, then yelled out the window, *"Does your mother know you're that stupid?"*

"She is not doing good. She barely sleeps. There's other stuff going on with her, you know."

"Like what?"

"Like . . . oh, just stuff. Anyway, I hear her up all hours of the night."

"Uh-huh, and what are you doing awake enough to hear her?"

"God, what are you, a shrink or something?"

Erica smiled. "I have to be, to keep up with Mr. Maestro Piano Genius." She pulled up to the curb in front of my building and checked her watch. We were actually a few minutes early. "Really, Mon. It's all gonna be fine. You have to get used to each other. Living together is harder than just being friends. But look at Ryan and me—we did it."

"It's not hardly the same thing."

"Sure it is. You guys just don't have sex."

"And you're suggesting you still do?" I grinned at her.

"Honey, you have no idea." She hit the auto unlock. "Now stop stressing and go to work, would you? All you need is some time, okay? You have to work at relationships. Nothing comes free."

✳ ✳ ✳

I thought about Erica that Friday night, as Samantha and I were getting ready to go to Noah's party. She and Ryan had been together almost five years now and they were actually still in love, so she was my new role model. She was twenty-two and had a college degree, and I figured she knew what she was talking about, seeing as their relationship had lasted longer than my mother's with my father. Besides, there was something about her and Ryan that just made me want to trust them. So, okay. Work at it, I would.

I'd finally chosen an outfit and was finishing up my make-up when Samantha cranked up Björk. The next thing I knew, she was prancing wildly around the apartment, in her underpants. "Hey! Turn that shit down, would you?" I called, but I was smiling. "And put some clothes on."

She poked her head in my bedroom door, stuck out her tongue at me, and kept dancing. This was Samantha like she'd been when we first moved in.

"Get a life, woman!" she taunted, and danced back down the hallway.

"Get a bra!" I yelled back.

"Envious of my large breasties, are you?" she cried, which set us both off laughing, because she was way too skinny and had no boobs at all. "Oh, very well."

"If I didn't know better," I told her, watching her strut toward the boys' place, "I'd say definite drug behavior."

"No. Fear, basically. I'm just covering."

"What are you afraid of?"

"Nothing, nothing. I'm just high on life, my dear. High on

life." She slowed and grabbed my arm. "Oh good. Look, all the really important people are here."

I smiled back at her as I checked out what she called "the asshole elite," the so-called beautiful people who managed to dress in bad gang clothes and still make it look like they had money. "Thank God, huh?"

"Mona, maybe we shouldn't go. We could just have everybody over some other time."

First, I laughed. Then, I realized she wasn't kidding. She was paler than ever. "What's wrong?"

"Shit. Me. I don't know."

"It's just a party, Samantha."

"Yeah, but . . . I don't know."

Of course she was thinking about Julie. I hesitated a second, then shrugged. "Hey. You want to go home? Let's go home. Fuck it." She threw me such a look of gratitude, I almost wanted to cry. But just as we started to turn around, Noah called to us from the top of the stairs.

"Mona! Sammie! Wait there, I'll be right down!"

I felt Samantha sigh. "We can still leave," I told her.

"No, it's okay. I'm fine. I just had a stupid moment there." She smiled. "It's okay. Really. High on life, remember?"

Inside was wall-to-wall people, and none of them looked younger than twenty-five.

"At least nobody'll throw up in the hall, right?" I whispered. Samantha just rolled her eyes. Noah's posters were hung all over the place, huge black-and-white close-ups of his face, and one of his whole body—in briefs. Samantha and I glanced at it, then at each other. Noah caught the look.

"Hey, you two. Stop that. It's my job."

"Heavens, No-ey, dahling, is that a bit of a blush I'm seeing there?" Andy asked, with a pseudo-English accent, coming up to us with beers in his hand. We each took one.

"I never blush," Noah countered.

"Too bad." Samantha actually winked at him. "I like men who do."

"Rub his cheek and see what happens," Erica said, coming up to give me a hug. She patted Noah's ass as she passed him, and we all laughed.

"Leave me alone, you guys," Noah said, but he obviously loved it.

I fully expected to be there for Samantha, the whole party if she needed me, so I stayed pretty close. We drifted around a bit, with Noah leading the way. Clearly, everybody loved our host. Especially the girls. He kept apologizing, but I noticed he didn't stop anyone from fawning all over him. Samantha actually went for a second beer. I started on my third and managed, for the most part, to keep her laughing. I kept looking for Daniel and finally found him, off in the corner with a girl who had more holes in her face than Swiss cheese.

"Think of the ones you can't see," Samantha whispered and I cringed. Still, they were talking very seriously. Just my luck.

"Don't worry. He's telling her he doesn't want to see her any-more," Erica whispered, seeing my expression. Erica and Ryan joined us just as Noah held out his hand to Samantha. She threw me a questioning look and I nodded, so she shrugged and went with him. Erica smiled at me and gave a little wink.

"Why not?" I asked, focusing back on Daniel. I wanted her to say, "Because he's in love with you."

"Who knows, with Daniel," Ryan told me.

"How long have they been going out?"

Erica giggled a little. "'Going out' is not exactly what they do together, if you get my drift."

"Okay. Gotcha." I stared at him again. He was almost as good-looking as Noah.

"Oh, by the way, we came to see if you wanna smoke some pot?" Ryan asked. Erica poked him, hard.

"That was diplomatic," she told him, then smiled at me. "Sorry. I don't even know if you smoke."

"That would be, um . . . yes." I must've grinned really hard because they both laughed. "Let's go!" I checked the room for Samantha, but she and Noah were nowhere to be seen. "Wait . . . maybe I should hang out until—"

"She's a big girl, Mona. She'll be fine," Erica assured me. "Come on."

Parties have a way of taking on a life of their own, and this one did just that. Ryan and Erica and I hung out in their room with a couple of his musician friends, and I completely lost track of time, listening to them talk about this band and that orchestra. I got to that amazing place where I could say or do damn near anything, but I wasn't out of control. Then one of the guys mentioned haircuts, and I thought of Samantha and started laughing.

"Shit," I explained as I scrambled up. "I forgot about my friend!" Of course, she was nowhere to be seen. No doubt she and Noah had realized they were absolutely perfect for each other. Now I had to think about me. Out of the corner of my eye, I saw Daniel glancing my way, so I dropped myself into a conversation with some guys close by. I laughed a lot and swung my hair around. When he edged over closer, I pretended I didn't notice him. The pierced girl had disappeared. But even though he had tons of other girls trying to get his attention, he kept sneaking peeks at me.

Samantha suddenly appeared beside me. "Can we go?"

"Sure. Where's Noah?"

"Who knows? Pissed, I guess."

"Uh-oh, what happened?"

"Nothing. Really. Where did you go?"

"With Ryan and Erica."

"Next time, tell me, okay?"

"I didn't know where you were."

"Okay. Let's just go, shall we?"

"Sure, let me go say bye to Noah. Do you know where he is?"

"Noah's here," said a male voice. I whirled and there he was, staring at Samantha. She turned her head away from him.

"Hi, we're leaving. Thanks for the party."

"I'll walk you home."

"That's okay," Samantha said, giving him the most incredibly evil smile I'd ever seen. "We'll be fine."

"Can we talk sometime?" he asked her.

"Why?" And before he could answer, she turned and I followed her to the door.

She didn't say a word all the way home.

"Shit, Samantha," I finally said, just as we shut the door to our apartment. "Are you going to tell me what happened?"

"Nothing happened."

"Right. I believe you. *Not.*"

"He's a jerk. Just like I knew he would be."

"What did he do?"

"It's not what he did. It's what he expects everybody else is gonna do. He thinks he's God's gift, you know what I mean?"

"Did he make some moves you didn't like?"

"Okay. I wouldn't kiss him, right? I mean, I barely know the guy. So guess what he said?" She snorted for emphasis. "'Don't be intimidated by my looks, babe.'"

"Omigod. What did you say?"

"I laughed, and told him I felt quite comfortable with egotistical, good-looking bastards."

"Go, girl."

"Yeah. And by the way, why did you desert me?"

"Wait a minute, hold on. You're the one who left."

"Yeah, then you disappeared."

"I was with Erica and Ryan. They had some pot. Then I looked for you."

"Right."

"I did! I told you, I thought you and Noah—"

"Whatever. It's okay. It doesn't matter. I'm sorry. I'm being a jerk. It's not your fault."

"No, I'm sorry."

"Okay, well, we both are."

"I can't believe he said that."

"I know. Me, either."

"It really upset you, huh?"

"No. I mean, yes. But it wasn't that. It was the whole thing. The party. I shouldn't have gone." She took a step back and stared so hard I thought her eyes were going to bore holes through me. But she wasn't really seeing me. She just happened to be facing in my direction. I put my hand on her arm, but she pulled away.

"Are you okay?" I asked.

She snapped back and smiled. "Yeah, I'm fine. Tired."

"It was just a party, you know?"

"I guess it was, huh?"

"Yeah. That's all." I started rubbing my temples. "Want something to eat?"

"No, thanks."

"Want to talk?"

"No. I just want to go to bed."

Which she did. And I sat and listened to her rustle around in her room and felt really stupid because I didn't know what to do or say, or anything. I knew that this wasn't all because of Noah. He wasn't that important. It had more to do with Julie; I could feel it. Maybe it was her first party since . . . and I just wasn't enough to take her mind off that. Or maybe she was mad because I went off and smoked pot. No doubt Julie didn't.

Twice, I went to her door and almost knocked. The third

time, I just put my ear close and listened. I expected to hear her crying or something, but there was nothing, no sound. Still, the room had that "awake" feeling; she definitely wasn't sleeping. I imagined her sitting there, by her window, staring out at the street. I went back out to the living room and turned on the TV, so she'd know I was up and maybe she'd come out and we could at least sit together. I might not know what to say to her about Julie, but at least I usually could make her laugh. But she didn't come out, and I fell asleep on the couch.

In the morning, it was like nothing ever happened.

Samantha

He was a short, round business type squished into a blue button-up shirt that made his neck bulge out over the top. I showed him to his seat without any hassle, but every time one of the waitresses passed, he leered at her. He called Gwyneth "honey" and couldn't take his eyes off her tits the whole time she was taking his order. She made a face in my direction and flipped him off on the sly, as she headed for the kitchen. I almost started to laugh, except that now he was leering at me. I managed to nod politely and forget about him completely as I concentrated on learning how to do this waitress thing.

I loved Malone's. Nobody knew anything about me, so however I acted was normal. I'd actually done okay as hostess, even though I was terrified I'd screw up, and of course, dreamed it, every night, the entire job, just like when I was a kid and got put in the advanced ballet class. Then, I'd done the variations, over and over, in my sleep, and would wake up exhausted. Now I took names, found seats, gave out menus, refilled condiments and rang up tabs. Waitressing was worse. I had to carry dishes, write orders, pour soft drinks, make salads, and most important, remember who got what and where they were sitting. Plus I had to be nice.

So I wasn't thinking about Fat Neck at all when I got stuck in front of his table. My hands were full of plates and I was frantically trying to recall who got the root beer and was it table twelve or thirteen that had ordered the steak sandwich. I didn't even realize where I was until he reached over and lightly rubbed my butt.

"Nice ass," he muttered, not actually looking at me.

I glanced back, but I wasn't completely sure he'd actually said anything. And I couldn't swear that he touched me on purpose, so I ignored him. The next thing I knew, he cupped my butt cheek with his hand, and squeezed.

"Watch it, asshole!" I spoke louder than I'd intended and as I jerked my body away from him, the plate with the steak sandwich and fries flew off the tray and shattered on the floor. Suddenly, there was plenty of space around me, and the entire restaurant was still. I squatted down to clean up the mess, feeling my face turn red. Fat Neck squinted his little pig eyes at me and stood.

"What did you say?" he demanded in a whiny voice.

"Nothing." I didn't look at him.

"I need the manager," he sputtered, swelling up like bread dough. Sal ambled over from behind the bar, wiping his hands on the towel tucked into the front of his pants, looking like an ancient busboy.

"I'm the owner," he said quietly.

Fat Neck puffed out even more. His voice stayed obnoxiously loud. "Your waitress was disrespectful."

"She was?" Sal flicked his eyes at me. I mouthed "I'm sorry," but he ignored it.

"Yeah." Fat Neck let his gaze swoop around the room, enjoying the drama and the attention. "And *I'd* like an apology." He crossed his short chubby arms and rocked back a little on his heels.

Sal smiled when he talked, but you got the sense he didn't mean it. "Can't do it, buddy." His voice was like a dog's growl before it bites. It was very low, but it carried. Everyone in the entire place could hear it. "I saw you touch the young lady."

"I beg your pardon!" Fat Neck sputtered, and I stood up, blushing even more.

"Twice. On her tush. So I think you're the one to apologize."

"How dare you?! I would never—"

"I saw you, too, *asshole,*" came a voice from my other side. It was the woman from table thirteen, and all of a sudden I remembered who was supposed to get the steak sandwich. Now it wasn't me at the center of attention, and Fat Neck suddenly had someplace he had to be. Shaking his head, he collected his jacket and tried to head for the door. Sal moved into his path.

"The young lady is waiting."

"She'll just have to wait, then, won't she?" Fat Neck muttered as he tried to push his way past. As short as he was, he was taller than Sal.

Smooth as silk, Frankie the bartender, who could have doubled as Mr. America, appeared behind Sal. Nobody spoke for a second, then Fat Neck slithered backward. Without once meeting my eyes, he murmured, "Sorry." Sal and Frankie stepped aside, and the other customers applauded as he scowled his way to the door. Waitresses were grinning like crazy, and Sal had to wave us all back to work.

"What? I'm paying you all to stand around?" He headed up toward his office. I caught him on the stairs.

"Sal, um, I'm really sorry . . ."

"You didn't do nothing wrong, kid. You're a good girl. You remember that. You also remember—there's a lot of assholes in the world." He gave me a thumbs-up and went on through the door.

And for some stupid reason, I felt like crying.

Mona made dinner. Things were getting back to normal now that my hours had changed. It wasn't quite like those giddy first days, when we couldn't get enough of just hanging out with each other, when we'd go out food shopping at midnight, just because we could. But it was nice.

"Okay," she announced as we both sat, cross-legged, on the living-room floor. She dished out the spaghetti and I broke the garlic bread. "We have to plan."

"Plan what?"

"The boys, stupid. What did you think?"

"Oh, 'the boys.' You couldn't possibly mean those arrogant asshole boys?"

"The very same."

"I'll pass, thanks." I wound the pasta onto my fork. "I told you what happened, Mona. He's not my type."

"So he made a mistake. It was probably just a line. I mean,

how was he to know you're not one of his bimbos?"

"Sorry. No way. He's far too important for me."

"Yeah, well. He called." She picked up a piece of bread and dipped it in the sauce. "Three times as a matter of fact. I told him you were busy."

"Next time tell him I died."

"I also happened to mention where you worked."

"Mona!"

"Oh come on. Are you going to tell me you don't like him just a little?"

"No. He's a shithead."

"So are you. So what?"

"I can't believe you did that."

"Well, if I left it to you, nothing would ever happen. Besides, he's really not that bad at all."

"Then you have him."

"I don't want him. I want Daniel."

"Another fine example of arrogant asshole."

"They're boys. What do you expect?" I couldn't help but grin. "Besides, he called me this morning. I pretended I couldn't quite place who he was."

"You did not."

"Oh yes I did. We're going out to dinner this Saturday."

"You lie."

"What Mona wants, my friend, Mona usually gets."

Later that night, after we'd giggled our way into exhaustion and tucked ourselves into our rooms, I heard a clanging outside, and got up to look. It was my old woman; her cart had run into the garbage can across the street. She froze like a cat in head-lights, then carefully looked one way, then the next. She glanced toward my window, but I made sure she couldn't see me. Finally, she walked around the cart twice, nodded and patted and went about her routine.

Mona

"Mom? Mom . . . I know it's you. Why don't you talk?" I looked helplessly over at Daniel and mouthed, "Just one minute."

Daniel smiled and wrapped his arms around my waist. Dinner had been awesome. Gently, I pushed him away, trying to keep from smiling too much. He came right back again, from behind, holding me with both arms. "Stop, please, okay?" I blew a kiss at him and this time he moved, settling himself in on the couch. "Mom? Come on. You can't keep hanging up on me. I know it's you. Just talk, please—" *Click.* I sighed once and slammed down the phone. "Damn."

Daniel smiled up at me. "Maybe you should call her back. You know how moms are."

"No shit." I went out to the kitchen. "But it's cool, I'll call her later. Want a beer?" He nodded.

"Dinner was great, huh?" he asked.

"Sure was." I opened the beer and brought it out to him. He patted the couch and I sat down. And all of a sudden I felt like I was fourteen again and still a virgin.

"You are so pretty," he said, taking a strand of my hair and pushing it back behind my ears. I felt my nipples get hard.

"Don't, okay?"

"Don't what, babe?" He ran his fingers down the side of my face.

"Just . . . don't."

"Sorry. Can't help myself."

"You're not staying tonight."

"I know. That's okay."

"We're not . . . you know. At least not now."

"I understand."

"So good. Let's just talk. Okay? You know what I mean? No need for any big seduction."

"Yes, ma'am." He saluted and grinned at me. "But you're still fucking beautiful."

We were in my room when Samantha got home, actually halfway through. I froze when I heard her key in the door. "Oh shit," I whispered. He smiled down at me, kissed me lightly on the forehead, and kept moving, very very slowly.

"Mona?" she called.

"In my room," I called back, holding up my fingers to my lips. Daniel mimed turning a lock on his. I heard her go to the kitchen, run some water and then head toward my door. "Um. I'm not alone." She stopped short.

"Oh." There was a second of silence. "But, you're okay?"

"Yeah," I said just as Daniel kissed me again. I giggled. "Completely."

"Uh-huh. Okay. Um. Do you want me to go out or something?"

"No, it's all right."

"Well, I'm going to, um, take a bath. A long one. With the radio playing."

Forty-five minutes later, I rapped on the bathroom door. I had to knock twice because she really *was* playing her music loud. When she opened the door, she was fully clothed, and stood there holding a book.

"You're not taking a bath."

"If I was, I'd be a prune by now." She glanced down the hall. "Is he gone?"

"Yeah."

"Daniel?"

"Who else?"

"Mona! You said you weren't going to."

"I didn't mean to, it just happened."

"I do not believe this." We both went out to the living room.

"I couldn't help it. Don't be mad."

"I'm not mad. It's just . . . Mona, you give in too easy."

"So what? So he never calls me again. I don't care." I noticed a vase full of roses on the counter. "What are those?"

"Flowers. From Noah. He sent them to Malone's."

"No shit. That's very cool." I glanced back at her, but she was still shaking her head. "Okay, fine. Make me feel even stupider than I already do. You get roses. I get fucked. Typical, huh?"

"Mona. I'm sorry. I'm sure it'll be all right."

I waved her away. "I told you, I don't care."

"Yes you do. And he'll be back. You watch."

"Right."

"He will." She sat down next to me on the couch. "You're

way too pretty. And sexy. And cool." She looked over at the door and back at me. "But how'd you get him to go home?"

"Never mind. It's really dumb."

"No, what did you say?"

"I told him thanks, that's all I really wanted, so he could go." She grinned at me. "You did not."

"Yeah, I did. And when he looked at me with those big brown eyes, I said, 'You've had my body, dear boy. Maybe someday you'll grow up enough to comprehend my mind.'"

"Oh shit."

We both busted out laughing. Until the phone rang and we froze. I made a face. "He couldn't be calling already. Could he?" I said, and Samantha shrugged. I turned away from the phone. "You get it. Say I'm sleeping."

"Hello?" A pause. Samantha shook her head no and then rolled her eyes in my direction. "No, Mrs. Brocato, I'm afraid she's asleep." I threw her a kiss. "What?" She rolled her eyes again. "Of course she's not alone. I'm here, too."

Samantha

I saw her downtown, on Geary. I had the day off and was on my way to meet Mona for lunch. I had decided to take streetcars instead of hassling with parking and was heading toward my transfer when all of a sudden—she came around the corner by Macy's. It couldn't be, but it was. I stopped so abruptly a father holding a baby ran into me. He cussed and the baby started to cry.

"Watch yourself, young lady," he cautioned.

"Sorry," I muttered without looking. I hustled through the lunchtime crowd and caught up with her turning down Powell, now almost a block ahead of me.

It was Jules. I'd swear it.

It was her broad shoulders and narrow waist, but mostly the way she stepped right out proud and tall, like a dancer, her long dark hair swinging across her back. No one else moved like that. I almost lost her in the crowd at the cable car turnaround, but managed to catch up as she waited to cross the street. When the light changed, I hurried ahead, held my breath, and whirled around.

I felt like someone socked me in the stomach. The woman

I'd been following was about thirty. And she didn't look at all like Jules.

Mona and I ended up at this little Mexican place that made huge, "healthy" burritos. It was crammed full of business people, but we managed to snag a booth in the very back. She started to catch me up on the ongoing saga of Daniel. Who *had* called and who was now very much a part of our lives. She was right in the middle of telling me her latest little power play with him, when she shook her head and crossed her arms.

"Okay. What's wrong?" she asked, interrupting herself.

"Nothing."

"Right. You've been on drugs since you came in."

"I'm . . . nothing. I don't know what you're talking about."

"Did Noah call?"

"Does he ever not?" I smiled a little. Noah had been waging an ongoing campaign for my attention. Roses showed up constantly, always red, always perfect—with very nice little notes. And he appeared in the flesh—either at Malone's, or dropping by when Daniel did. Sal had started calling him "your young man." And I had to admit that Mona had been right; he wasn't really as bad as I first believed.

"Okay. If it's not Noah and you don't do drugs, then what's wrong? Did you hear from your mom? Your dad? My mom? The Pope? What? Come on, something's going on."

I almost told her. I almost opened my mouth and said, *It's November twentieth and that's Jules's birthday and I've been trying to ignore the fact for weeks but I can't and I even thought I saw her this morning and what's scary is that I really did believe it was her. And*

*what's even scarier is that right now, this very minute, I am thinking
about her and I am not feeling anything. Nothing. Not a teeny bit of
sadness or grief. And I never do, not anymore. I don't feel like crying.
If I miss her, I can't tell. She's just there, every once in a while, in my
mind, stuck in ice. I can see her and I remember things, but it's like
I'm remembering somebody that I barely knew.*

Because I feel nothing.

*And it's weird and I don't understand it. And there's no fucking
way in the world I can tell anyone—especially not you.*

Instead, I managed a little smile and said a different truth.
"Well, okay, you're right. It's Noah. I think maybe I'm starting to
like him."

She shrieked, and the whole group of suits at the next
table turned their heads toward us. "I knew it, I knew it, I
knew it. . . . You two are perfect. Omigod, let's have them over,
let's do something . . . yeah? Okay?"

"Not right this minute, okay? Let me just call him back once
or twice first. I mean, he may not want it if he knows he can
have it, you know what I mean?"

Around six o'clock that night, just before Mona was due
home from work, I called Sandra. I wasn't exactly sure what I
was going to say, but it seemed like the right thing to do. Rosie
answered.

"Hello, who is it, please?" I smiled. Jules used to answer the
phone the same way, when we were ten.

"Hey, Punky, it's Sammie."

"Sammie! Where have you been? Did you go away?"

"Yeah, I moved. To San Francisco."

"It's Julsie's birthday today."

"I know."

"But she's not here anymore," Rosie announced, her almost six-year-old voice sounding strangely old.

That was unexpected. I took a quick breath. "Well, how are *you*?"

"Good. I'm in first grade. I have homework. And I do not like boys."

"Uh-oh. Not even Andrew?" I teased. Andrew had been her closest friend since preschool.

"Nope. You do not like boys in first grade."

"Got it." I smiled as I imagined her little body shifting as she talked. "So, is Mommy or Daddy home?"

"Daddy doesn't live here right now."

"Oh." I couldn't quite get my mind around that one, either. Sandra and William were the one couple who would always be together. I sighed again. "Okay."

"But we're not divorced. We're just taking some time off."

"Well, that's a good thing. So can I talk to your mom?"

"I don't think so. She's in Julsie's room, crying."

It took everything I had to keep from hanging up. "Okay, I'll call her later. And you take care—"

"Sammie?" There was an awkward little pause and suddenly Rosie sounded like a little girl again. "Will you come see me sometime?"

"Of course I will. Or you can come see me here."

"Okay." Rosie lowered her voice. I got the definite idea she did not want her mother to hear her. "But Sammie, can I ask you a question?"

"Sure. Anything."

"You know how Mommy said Julsie went up to heaven?"

"Yeah."

"Well, do you know when she's coming home?"

I took a deep breath and pulled it together to speak. "No, Rosie, I don't. But I sure wish it would be soon."

"Yeah. Me, too. You promise to come over?"

"I promise, Punky."

Mona

"We're lost," Samantha announced, craning her head up and around to get a better look. We sat at an intersection: one endless two-lane street with dirt on both sides crossed another that looked exactly the same. Neither one had street signs. She and I were smooshed in the back seat of the Jeep, since Daniel insisted he couldn't fit. Noah was driving. "Some Thanksgiving," she continued, with a sideways wink at me. "I knew we shouldn't have let you talk us into this."

"It happened to be your idea," Noah insisted. "And we are not lost."

"Hello? What would you know? You're from L.A.," I shot back. "They do not have streets like this in Los Angeles."

"She's right, you know," Samantha added, looking around again. She patted Noah on the side of the head. "Good thing you have a pretty face."

Daniel turned around to stare at us for a second. Then he turned to Noah. "Do you hear this?" he asked. "Do you hear these women?" He shook his head. "I can't believe it. No respect. No faith. That's the problem these days. Girls have absolutely no faith." He kicked back, folding his arms behind his head. "Drive on, Noah-man. I trust you."

"You should have let Samantha drive," I said.

"Yeah, *I* can read a map at least."

"Men don't need maps," Daniel assured us.

I poked Daniel's shoulder. "Then he should have asked that guy at the gas station."

"Men never ask directions," Daniel replied.

Samantha added, "Which is exactly why we're lost."

"We are not lost," Noah muttered. "I know where I am."

"Uh-huh. Oh, Noah, look. Over there." Samantha pointed toward the field. "See? Those are cows." She spread her hands. "But where's Marine World? I thought we were going to Marine World."

"Men like cows," I explained. "Makes 'em feel like cowboys."

We burst out laughing and Noah scowled, then looked both ways, twice, and turned left. He turned left again, and then right, and finally got onto a freeway named 37.

"Well, at least we'll be able to get home," Samantha teased, pointing to a sign that said SAN FRANCISCO.

"Oh, ye of little faith," Daniel answered. Noah just kept driving.

"There!" Noah sat up tall and pointed to a trio of huge roller coasters that appeared as we turned the corner. A sign over the freeway said: MARINE WORLD, AFRICA USA. He held up his hand and Daniel slapped five.

"You just got lucky," I chided.

"Luck had nothing to do with it, my dear," Noah announced

as he made the turn. But I caught the "thank-God" look he gave Daniel, and elbowed Samantha. She nodded and winked.

"Okay, who's paying?" I said, pulling away from Daniel and heading for the gate.

Samantha trotted alongside. "The *men*, of course." She slipped her arm through mine and we ignored the protests from behind us. "God, I wish I had your tits," she whispered.

"Trade ya for the legs."

The boys paid, grumbling all the way, and inside, Daniel claimed his place next to me and Noah kind of shyly took Samantha's hand. I just smiled. This was her and Noah's first actual "date." She hadn't lost any time; the very day after she'd confided in me about liking him, he was over for dinner. We ate, we talked, we watched a movie, and then Samantha had ushered him out the door, without so much as a kiss good night. I don't know who was most surprised—Daniel, Noah, or me. Samantha had just smiled her perfect smile.

"That's a first," Daniel had whispered to me as we headed for my room. "Poor Noah."

"He'll cope," I told him.

And he did, by sending her candy with her next dozen roses. And here we were, on Thanksgiving, at Marine World. We explored, played games, ate tons of junk food, and finally waited in line for the Great White Whale show. "What are all these people doing here?" Daniel grumbled. "Don't they know it's a holiday?"

"Sit down front. We'll only get a little wet," Noah ordered when we finally got in, and shushed Samantha when she started to protest.

The whales, Duncan and Zack, did incredible tricks with their trainers—carrying them, tossing them, swimming under the surface right alongside them—and Noah was right, we did only get a little wet. Then came the finale. Duncan disappeared to the holding tank while the larger whale, Zack, raced around the arena, faster and faster, until it seemed the whole thing was a whirlpool. Suddenly, his trainer held his arms straight up and Samantha ducked down a little. Zack dove deep under the water and then soared straight up into the air.

"Ah, shiiii—" was all Daniel could get out before Zack hit the pool and sent the entire contents directly onto us. "Wet" didn't begin to describe it. I reached over and smacked Noah.

"What? What'd I do?" he asked, hunched over with laughter.

"You knew this would happen!" I said. I punched Samantha lightly. "You did, too!"

By the time we were ready to leave, the sun was already starting down. The air got very cold. We climbed into the Jeep and all four of us huddled, still damp, in the blankets Samantha kept in the back, as we waited for the park traffic to thin out. Stars were everywhere. "Now this is something to be thankful for," I murmured.

"No kidding. Why do we live in San Francisco?" Samantha asked.

"I don't know, but I don't want to go back," I replied, cuddling closer to Daniel.

"Okay, let's spend the night up here," Noah suggested.

"Sorry, didn't bring my sleeping bag," Samantha said, "and it's too damn cold to—"

"I meant—at a hotel." He held up his Visa card. "My treat."

Samantha

Daniel and Noah were doing their Adam Sandler routine. Mona was laughing way too loudly and obviously didn't give a shit that *I* wanted to go back to San Francisco. We'd had a great time, but I was tired and cranky and I wanted to be in my own apartment, in my own bed—alone. Instead, I was speeding down another stupid two-lane "highway" going God-knows-where with a bunch of crazy horny people. I didn't want to be the "bad guy," and I still had hope this would die a natural death; the two places we'd passed so far both looked like the Bates Motel.

Then the highway got bigger, and an Embassy Suites appeared in a cluster of trees.

"That's us," Noah announced and took the next off-ramp.

It was now or never. But Mona kept babbling on about the swans in the atrium, the gazebo next to the outdoor pool, and the free breakfast in the morning, and I never did get the words out. The next thing I knew we were on the top floor in a suite with a fold-out couch in the living room and a king-size bed in the bedroom. It was one of their best rooms, and Noah got a deal. Apparently, most people in Napa don't stay in hotels on Thanksgiving.

Daniel ordered room service pizza and two bottles of what he insisted was very expensive champagne. He was practically drooling on Mona—who was definitely drooling back. I'd caught the look of conquest he and Noah flashed each other on the way up in the elevator and was feeling like I was thirteen again—with everybody but me having a good time.

Room service arrived. Mona sidled up as the boys hustled about getting the dining room area set up.

"Is this place great or what?" she whispered.

"It's a bit much for a first date."

"Samantha . . ."

"What? I'm not going to say anything."

"Good, 'cause I kinda want to be here."

"Just know I'm not sleeping with Noah, okay?"

She noticed the boys checking us out and smiled. "Well, you're certainly not sleeping with me."

Daniel popped the champagne cork and we both jumped. He poured and Noah passed us each a glass.

"To Thanksgiving," Daniel toasted.

"And beautiful women," Noah added, tipping his glass toward me. I held up my glass for the toast and with a smile at him and then Mona, gulped down the entire thing.

"Thirsty, huh?" Noah asked, winking as he reached for the bottle to pour me some more champagne. I winked back as he settled in next to me on the couch, and suddenly found it very funny that he'd probably be spending the night on the chair, when he obviously assumed he'd be getting together with me.

"Do you realize we didn't even know you two last year?" He passed the bottle to Mona, who'd also finished her glass.

"Hell, we didn't know each other," I announced, as Daniel pulled Mona onto his lap and bit her neck, making her giggle.

"Wait a minute," Noah said. "I thought you guys grew up together."

"Didn't even meet the girl until this past summer," I told him. Mona shifted away from Daniel and almost rudely glared at me. I wasn't sure why I was pissing her off, but obviously I had. I chugged again.

"Whoa, girl," Noah said, "it's stronger than it looks."

"But oh so good," I argued, sipping this time. I was actually starting to enjoy myself.

"*We've* known each other since kindergarten," Daniel bragged.

"Oh wow, I'm impressed," I said, teasingly. "That's amazing."

"You wouldn't think that if you had to spend every holiday with him," Noah said.

"I didn't hear you complaining last Christmas," Daniel challenged. "When I brought Christina and Kaitlyn along."

Mona gave Daniel a look to kill. I started to giggle. "Uh-oh," I said, and elbowed Noah. "Busted."

"They were just friends," Daniel said.

"Sure they were." Mona pouted and stood up. She plopped herself down on the couch next to me.

"So what were you doing?" Noah asked. Daniel got up to open the second bottle. He tried his puppy dog eyes on Mona, but she wasn't paying attention.

"I was dodging turkey," Mona said.

"Excuse me?" Noah asked.

"It's an old Italian family tradition," Mona assured him, in a serious, matter-of-fact tone. "Your mother takes hold of the drumstick and tries to smack you in the head." I practically snorted champagne through my nose, laughing.

"I don't get it," Daniel said, as he popped the second cork.

"I'm not talking to you," Mona said.

"I don't get it, either," Noah said.

"It's very simple, *Noah*. I was playing 'functional family' with my crazy mother," she explained. "On the other hand, Samantha—" she patted my knee and smiled—"was probably with *Jules*, right? No doubt doing something incredibly normal."

I froze for a second. I couldn't believe Mona had just said that.

"Who's Jules?" Daniel asked.

"I'm sorry, did someone speak?" Mona asked Noah. Daniel did the eyes again, and mouthed "please?" and this time she gave in. She joined him on their chair.

"*Jules* is Samantha's best friend," she said, sitting back on his lap, with a sassy little smile.

I set my glass down on the table in front of me, wishing now I hadn't finished the second one. Mona had just opened that door my mother liked so much—the one that didn't affect anyone else in the world except me. Jules was gone. I was here. It was getting hard to think straight.

"I thought *you* were her best friend," Noah said, looking from her to me.

Mona babbled on. I wouldn't let myself believe she knew how much this hurt. "Nope. That'd be *Jules*."

I stood so abruptly I almost knocked over Noah's champagne. "Shit," he exclaimed, "what'd I do?"

"Sorry," I muttered. "Her name is Julie," I hissed at Mona.

"Right. I knew that. Her name is *Julie,* guys!" She leered at me, obviously shit-faced, and then curled herself up onto Daniel. "Julie, Julie, Julie. *Or . . .* you can say Juliana! Right? But not Jules. Don't ever say Jules."

"Maybe you could let it go, huh?"

"I'm just trying to tell the guys about Julie—"

"Who is not their business, okay?" I wanted to slap her and get the hell out of here.

"Okay," Mona slurred. "Okay, I got it. I will not talk about her."

"Talk about who?" Daniel asked.

"Yeah . . . who's this Julie person?" Noah piped in.

Mona put her finger to her lips and shook her head. "No, no, no. We didn't even know each other last year. So no more talking about Julie."

"Where are my keys?" I demanded, then saw them on the counter and snatched them.

"Oh, come on," Daniel begged. "I wanna hear about her."

"Uh-oh, now I did it," Mona whined. "Don't leave. I was just playing."

I couldn't trust myself to answer. I bolted through the door. Thoughts were whipping about entirely too fast now, and my head was fuzzy from the alcohol. I didn't know if I wanted to scream or run myself into a wall. I couldn't remember where the elevator was, so I took the stairs I found in the corner and finally got myself outside. I had no idea where my car was parked, but suddenly, it didn't matter because I had to throw up. I hid myself in the bushes and let it all go.

Afterward, I wanted to cry, but I couldn't. I wasn't a bit drunk anymore and couldn't figure out why I had let such a stupid thing make me crazy. My mouth tasted nasty and my head was starting to throb. But I was not at all willing to go back upstairs to the room. The three of them could think what they wanted; I didn't really care. Who were these people to me, anyway? I just needed to find my car and get home.

"Sneaking out, huh?" Noah's voice startled me. He came jogging up from behind. "You just gonna leave us here?"

"I'll pick you up tomorrow." I kept walking. I'd spotted my Jeep.

"Hey, slow down, I've been running all over the place looking for you. We need to talk."

"There's nothing to talk about."

"Mona told us about Julie."

"Mona would." We reached the car and I climbed in the front. Noah got in the passenger side.

"I'm really sorry, Sammie."

"Well, there's nothing you can do about it, is there?" I started the car and turned my head to Noah. "Bye. Time to get out." He shook his head and fastened his seat belt.

San Francisco was almost an hour and a half away, and most of it we drove in silence. Noah lay back and kept the music flowing. I concentrated on keeping the Jeep on the road. There were no lights at all along the Black Point cutoff—and tonight, not many cars, either. Just darkness and the yellow reflectors that divided one side from the other. The endlessness of it was eerie, but soothing—except for a brief moment when I felt like there was something scary out there in the dark. I glanced at Noah and he smiled back at me. He never said a word though, not until we got back to the city.

"I'm coming up," he announced, as I parked in front of my building, "and putting you to bed."

"Forget about it," I blurted. "I'm not sleeping with you."

"I didn't expect you would. But you also don't need to be alone."

He fixed food while I cleaned up. We finally landed on the couch, watching a marathon of old *X-Files*. Neither one of us mentioned Mona or Jules or anything about the evening. I relaxed and we cuddled, and somewhere in the early morning, he kissed me. It was soft and slow and he didn't even put his arms around me, just gently touched the side of my face. I could pull away easily, but I didn't want to. He pressed his lips to my neck, then slowly started to unbutton my shirt. I could feel my body begging to let him do it, but I shook my head no and pulled away. I watched his eyes clear as he focused.

"Want to stop?" he whispered.

I nodded.

"You sure?"

"Uh-huh." I wasn't at all.

"Okay." He sucked in a deep breath. "Okay. That's fine." He sat up and grinned a little sheepishly as he adjusted his pants. "Just give me a second, all right?" He stood, and I could see the bulge in the front. I tried unsuccessfully not to blush. He looked down at himself and laughed. "I think I'll get some . . . oh, I don't know—cold water?"

I could hear him in the bathroom and then whistling his way to the kitchen. I turned off the TV and sat back on the couch. At least I'd been consistent this evening, first making a fool of myself at the hotel, and then again here with Noah.

"Come on," he said, from the hallway. "Let's go to bed." He held out his hand. "To *sleep*, okay? Just to sleep."

Then the most stupid of all things—I started to cry. Not big sloppy real tears, just trickles, but I didn't know why and I couldn't stop.

"Oh, honey . . . " Noah said in the softest, sweetest voice I'd ever heard. "Oh, sweetie, come here." He held his arms out and there really wasn't anything else to do but go into them.

Then we were on the bed together, holding each other. He stroked my hair and touched my face, then kissed me even more gently than before. Every part of my body responded.

"You're perfect," he whispered, laughing softly. "You are just plain perfect."

Everything changed to slow motion. I got worried for a second that I wouldn't know what to do, but it didn't really matter. I closed my eyes.

After, Noah wrapped me up in his arms.

I drifted toward sleep. *I'll have to tell Jules,* I thought, *it doesn't really hurt at all.*

Mona

This is the kind of shit that happens to me. I want to do something nice, like take some chicken soup over to my boyfriend, who has been home sick with this weird kind of flu. So, I ask for time off work, *not* a fun proposition when you have to get permission by lying to the infamous Mrs. Kiff about why you need a personal day. But I do it. Then I buy the very best soup I can find from Elly's Deli and put it into one of Samantha's mom's Tupperware things so it seems like I actually made it myself. I spend almost an entire hour getting myself together so I look as cute as I can without seeming that I'm trying to. Then, just as I'm about to go out the door, the phone rings. And stupid me answers it.

"Oh, Ramona, I'm so glad I found you!" My mother's voice is raspy, the way it gets when she's on her way down. "Can you come over? I'm here all alone."

"Hi, Mommy," I say, with that bright note that comes so naturally it makes me cringe. "How are you?"

"I'm alone. That's how I am. I want you to come and see me."

"Well, actually, I have to be at work soon." Still chipper,

playing good old Mona, hoping past hope that this will do it.

"Oh, Ramona." She's pleading now. "Please don't lie to me. I already called there. They said you took a day off." Her voice changes again, to exactly the tone she knows will get me. "Please, Ramona. Please come see me today. Just for a little while. Please?"

And so what did I do? I went. I drove over the bridge and went to her house and spent almost the whole damn day being exactly the kind of daughter I was supposed to be. I cleaned the entire place, which was filthy. I took her laundry down to the laundromat and did two loads. I drove her to do her food shopping, got those "chicken helper" things and made up three of them for the freezer. And all the time I raged inside, wishing I knew how to get myself out of it. But my sweet voice never deserted me, not even once. The "it's the disease" song kept playing over and over in my head. Somehow, I managed to talk her into going over to Aunt Mollye's, and then I fought the traffic to get back home.

Almost four o'clock. My stomach was hurting, I was so pissed. But Daniel was still sick and there was the soup. I heated it up and called over to make sure he was still home.

"Hello?" A girl's voice answered.

My skin turned icy. "Who's this?"

"Who's *this*?" she chirped.

"Erica?" It didn't sound like her, but I asked anyway. The girl hung up. I called immediately back. This time, it rang several times and then Daniel's voice came on the line. He sounded sleepy.

"'Lo?"

"Who was that?" I asked, pretty close to drowning in fear.

"Who was what?" he said, yawning.

"I just called, and some girl answered."

"You called just now?"

"Yeah."

"I didn't hear it, I guess. I was sleeping."

"Who else is there?"

"Um, I don't know. I don't think anybody is." He yelled away from the phone, "Anybody home?" Then he came back on. "Nope. Just me."

"You sure?"

"Why are you interrogating me? You should be helping me. I'm a sick boy. Come take care of me."

I paused a second, considering. No doubt I'd misdialed. "I'm on my way."

Samantha

"Watch out," Gwynnie warned when I got to work. "He's on the rag today."

"It's Laura's birthday," Chloe explained in a whisper. "He's always like this." I looked from one to the other and Chloe continued. "Laura was his wife. She died."

"Oh shit, I didn't know," I whispered back.

"It was thirteen years ago."

Just then, Sal came waddling around the corner. Gwynnie and Chloe immediately scrambled back to work. "Again?" Sal asked, glancing at me and down at his watch. "What? You got no life? Where's the boyfriend?"

"Working, I guess." I shrugged and winked at him. "Besides, I'd rather hang out with you."

"Well, come on upstairs. I got some office stuff you can do. But don't expect no overtime."

Fifteen minutes later, I peeked at him from behind the invoices he'd asked me to file. He looked grayer than usual, and the circles under his eyes were especially dark. He caught me looking.

"Yeah? What's so interesting?"

"You okay?"

"'Course I am. You're the one we should worry about."

I worked in silence for a few minutes, but the words wouldn't stay inside. "Chloe told me about Laura."

Sal didn't change what he was doing, but his face darkened and it took him a few seconds to answer. "Chloe ought to keep her mouth shut."

"I'm sorry, Sal."

He waved me away with his hand. "Yeah, you, me, everybody's sorry. You gonna work or not?"

I nodded and turned my attention to the bills.

Two hours later, I was still thinking about it. But this was "pick your own oldies night" and by eight, the place had gotten so busy, I could barely keep up with the crowd. It was a great concept—Sal got a DJ, and people could bring in whatever they wanted and he'd shove it into the mix. There was every kind of music imaginable, from Pink to the Drifters to Beck to the Beatles. I was loving it, dancing along with the beat, enjoying how well I could do this waitress stuff now.

Then, while I was taking an order, Rickie Lee Jones came on.

You saved your own special friend . . .
'Cause here, you need something to hide her in . . .
And you stay inside that foolish grin,
When every day now, secrets end,
Oh and then again, years may go by . . .

I hadn't heard this song since our dance concert last May. One second I was fine, writing down "2 prime ribs"; the next, I was backing away from the couple at the table, who, for some reason, kept talking. Jessie saw me and came over. Her eyes asked the question, but I just shook my head. She took my order pad and turned me toward the back door. I slipped outside and started to cry.

"What's going on, kid?" Sal's crusty old voice startled me. Jessie must have called him. I swiped at my eyes but couldn't quite manage to stop the flow.

"Nothing." Tears kept leaking out. This was stupid. Why was I crying now? I hadn't cried on her birthday.

He handed me a handkerchief and I blew my nose. "Sniffing those onions again, huh?"

I shook my head and tried to smile.

"You broke up with the boyfriend? That's why you came in early?" He waited a second, but I couldn't answer. "Look, if it was me, I'm sorry. I'm just an old ass sometimes."

"No. It's not you. . . . " I couldn't hold back the tears. "I just—"

"Hey. Hey. You don't got to say nothing."

I looked down at his face, into those ancient blue eyes inside all those wrinkles. "My friend died, Sal. And the song reminded me of her. That's all."

For a second our eyes locked, and it felt like that night I'd stared at the old woman. Too much that I didn't understand. "I'm sorry, Sammie. I didn't know." He turned gruff again, distant, not able to look directly at me. "Remember, it takes a while," he muttered. "It ain't easy. Just do the best you can."

"What do you mean?"

"Nothing. Never mind. Just old man talk." He patted my shoulder brusquely and gave me a fresh handkerchief. "You wanna go home?"

I shook my head no.

"You wanna talk to one of the girls?"

I shook my head again and even managed to almost smile. He nodded, patted my arm one more time and shuffled toward the door. Just before he went in, he looked over once again. "You sure?"

"I'm fine." There was only one person I wanted to talk to, and I never could.

Mona

We got a tree. We borrowed ornaments from both our moms and put them on, drinking eggnog with some really expensive rum I managed to score from the mailroom guy at work. We wrapped presents. We baked my special Extreme Chocolate Nut Cookies, a polite two dozen for Mrs. Kiff and then a whole bunch for Samantha to take to Malone's. One night, we drove around to look at Christmas lights. I pretended I didn't care that Daniel had finals and was all of a sudden too busy to come over and spend time with me. And somehow we managed to get up to Christmas Eve. We fixed a fancy chicken dinner and drank more eggnog spiked with rum. Ryan and Erica dropped by and—Merry Christmas, how lucky can you be?—the boys both showed up around nine o'clock. With gifts.

Samantha got a black turtleneck sweater, very expensive, and Daniel gave me a nightgown from Victoria's Secret. We went to bed around one but did hardly any sleeping. Which was just fine with me.

At breakfast, however, Daniel told me he was going to Colorado with Noah for a week. We were invited, which was lovely, except for the small fact that both of us had to work.

"Did you know this?" I asked Samantha, as we cleaned up the breakfast dishes. The boys were long gone.

"Sort of. I think Noah said something last week."

"And this is okay with you?"

"Actually, it doesn't really bother me."

"Come on. We never get to see them and now they're going skiing without us."

"Yeah, well, dancers don't ski. You could do permanent damage."

I gave her a look, but she didn't notice. "You know, this is the first time you've ever referred to yourself as a dancer?"

"Yeah?" She answered, but barely.

I wondered, as I had for the past three weeks, if she was still pissed off at me. We had never even talked about Thanksgiving. I mean, I'd tried to, but I only got as far as "I'm really sorry, Samantha," before she'd waved me away.

"It's no big deal, Mona," she'd insisted. "Really. I over-reacted."

When I told Erica about it, and about Julie, she was quiet for a minute, then counseled me to leave it alone. "Everybody grieves their own way, Mona," she explained.

"Except she's not grieving. She's ignoring."

"Well, that's the way some people are. Give it time."

So Christmas Day, after the boys left, we were like two strangers occupying the same space. Nothing was wrong, but nothing connected either. She was obviously preoccupied with thoughts of her own, and I was too bummed out about Daniel to pursue it.

"Do you think they're up there alone?" I blurted an hour or so after they'd gone.

"You mean, are they with other girls?"

"Yeah. Exactly."

"Does it really matter?"

"Of course it does."

"Why? If they want to dump us, they will. If they don't, they won't. Who cares if they fool around?"

"You do not really mean this."

"I'm not in love with Noah, Mona."

"Could have fooled me."

She shrugged. "I'm not. So I don't really care."

"Yeah, well, I'm not in love with Daniel, either. But I do not like being manipulated."

"Stop obsessing on this."

"I am *not* obsessing."

"Fine. Whatever."

We dragged through the rest of the morning and into the afternoon, ending up surfing from bad TV movie to bad TV movie. Suddenly, Samantha clicked off the tube.

"I have to go to Marin," she announced.

"Why?"

"I can't not see my mom."

"Did you tell her you'd come?"

"No, but it's Christmas." She stood up. "You're supposed to hang out with your family, right? Besides, I cannot sit around here one more second with nothing to do."

I didn't hesitate. "Can I go?"

* * *

We got all the way over to Mill Valley without talking. It wasn't a mad silence; it wasn't anything. We were both lost in our own heads.

Only holidays felt like this. I put in an old Beatles tape and thought about Samantha and the boys. She was right, but shit, how could you *not* care if someone you were with was with somebody else? I sneaked a glance at her as she drove. There was so much about her I simply did not understand.

"Okay, put on your Christmas spirit," Samantha muttered as we turned on to her street. But when we pulled up to the house, it was dark. Nobody was home. "Well, shit. I should've known."

"Want to go by Bruce's?"

"They won't be there either, betcha. I mean, why would you stay home on Christmas when you do something normal like gambling in Lake Tahoe?" She threw me a look, but I couldn't tell if she was pissed or what. "That's what they did last year."

"Uh, want to go see your Dad?"

"I don't think so. He's pretty much done his dad-thing for the decade."

"Okay, so now what?" I asked. "You want to visit friends or something?"

"I have no friends, Mona. Only you. So . . . let's go to your house."

"Sure, why not? *My* family's certainly normal. Whoops. Maybe not. But you're right, at least she'll be home."

"Good. Maybe I could even go inside this time?" she suggested.

"Don't be such a shithead."

"Why not? Everybody else is."

"Not me. I'm the asshole, remember?" I cocked my head at her. "You Shithead, me Asshole?"

Mom was there, along with my uncle Ford and my aunt Mollye, who met us at the door.

"She's not having one of her best days, Mona," Aunt Mollye explained. "You know how she gets around Christmas."

From behind me, I heard Samantha whisper, "Should I get ready to duck?" and I felt her giggles.

Somehow I managed to stay focused. "Yes, ma'am, I sure do. Did she see us drive up?" Mollye shook her head no. "All right. Then why don't I just call her next week sometime?"

"That's probably best."

"Damn," Samantha whispered as we headed back to the car. "I was hoping she was gonna throw some chicken." I punched her and we laughed ourselves back into the car, then had to sit a moment to recover. But when we looked at each other, we burst out laughing again.

"Merry Christmas, Samantha!" I sputtered.

"Merry Christmas to you, Mona!" she sputtered back. Finally, we wound down and both of us sighed.

"Okay," I asked, still holding my stomach. "Now I have to pee."

"It's a long way back to San Francisco."

"I don't suppose there'd be gas stations open?"

She shook her head no. "Can't think of one." She nodded her head toward the side. "Bushes?"

We ended up going to Denny's and having their Christmas Day special—processed turkey with processed gravy. It was the perfect ending for the day.

"Now what?" I asked as we paid the bill.

"I don't know. I don't think we have any more family around." We walked back out to the Jeep.

"Well. Do you, you know, I mean . . . " I sighed, trying to get my words together. "I thought maybe you might want to go see Julie." We climbed into the Jeep. "People do, you know. I just want you to know, I mean, if you do . . . I'd be happy to go with you."

She stared at me for a long time and then smiled and shook her head. "No. I don't think so. But thanks anyway."

It was quiet again and we headed back toward the bridge. Just as we were almost to it, I blurted, "Shit, Samantha, I'm so sorry. I can't seem to ever say the right thing."

"It's okay, Mona. It was a good idea. I'm just not into that kind of stuff. I'd rather remember her my own way."

"Well, just so you know. And if you ever want to talk about her . . ."

"Yeah. Thanks."

Samantha

We started by wishing for toe shoes and curly hair. Cuddled together on the couch in the den at her house, we hooked pinkies and squeezed our eyes shut. The TV blared as William and Sandra counted down with the ball in New York's Times Square. At exactly midnight, we touched our foreheads together and whispered our chant:

This we need most this year . . .

Pink toe shoes and curly hair.

We were ten. It was the first New Year's Eve we'd spent together. The next year we wished for my parents not to fight so much. After that, it was either boys or solos in our dance company, or both. Two years ago, we'd been to a party, but just before midnight, we snuck into an empty bedroom, held pinkies and chanted:

This we need most this year . . .

Forever always to be friends.

Someone in the next stall was throwing up their night's celebration. I heard the music stop in the other room and the countdown begin, and then everybody started singing "Auld Lang Syne." The entire bathroom reeked of cigarettes. The woman from next door started washing her face. I took a long, deep breath and exhaled slowly. Noah and Daniel were in Colorado. Mona was in major depression. My mother was getting married. Sandra was getting divorced. Jules was dead.

Happy New Year, everybody.

"Hey, you almost done in there?" Somebody rapped at the door of my stall. I flushed to make it more realistic and tried to smile as the woman pushed past me. Then I ventured back out to the floor. Mona grabbed me from behind; she was lit up and almost knocked me over. She was working tonight; Sal hired extra on New Year's Eve.

"Where were you?" she whispered in this intense tone of voice.

"Peeing. Damn."

"Noah and Daniel are here." She pointed, just as Noah called my name and headed toward us.

"Guess who we met in Aspen?" he gushed, talking loudly to be heard in the din. He dropped one arm around a pretty dark-haired girl and the other around a guy just as good-looking as he was. Daniel stayed by the door. Mona gestured for him to join us, but he acted like he didn't see her. "This is Ron. And this is Olivia." Noah smiled and then waited, as if this was supposed to elicit some kind of reaction.

"Hi." I glanced over to where Gwyneth was frantically waving at me. "Mona, can you find them a seat? I've got customers."

"Don't you recognize these people?" I heard Noah whisper to Mona as I walked off. She obviously did, but kept looking over toward Daniel as she led them to their table. There was quite a stir as other people realized who they were. Mona stopped on the way to get them drinks.

"I know, I know," I muttered before she could explain anything. "They're TV stars. I got it right off."

"Well, shit, that's pretty cool, don't you think? But what the fuck's wrong with Daniel?"

"What did he say?"

"Nothing; he's ignoring me."

"So ignore him back."

"I will." But she looked over with such longing, I doubted she could.

Noah found us a second later. "Hey, forget the drinks, we're leaving."

"You just got here," Mona said.

"Yeah, well, Ron and Livie want to see our place, and I don't know . . . this is not really my idea of how to spend New Year's Eve."

"'Livie'?" I muttered to Mona. She rolled her eyes.

"You should've told us you were going to be back," she snapped at him.

"Who knew?" Noah shrugged and gave me a kiss on the cheek. I pulled away. "Come on, don't be mad. It's New Year's Eve."

"Happy New Year's."

"Will we see you tomorrow?" Mona asked.

"Actually, no," he muttered. I shot him a quick sidelong look. "I'm going to LA for a few days."

"Have fun," I said, and picked up my tray.

"You can come if you want," he offered. I grinned and shook my head no.

"Is Daniel going?" Mona asked.

"Nope, he'll be here." He smiled at me. "This is kind of a business thing for me, you know."

"Absolutely. I understand. Hollywood calls." I started grabbing dirty glasses and stacking them on my tray.

Noah made a little pouty face. "What's your problem?"

"Just go, Noah," I said. "You're way too important for me tonight."

"Sammie . . ."

Just then, Ron called out, "Hey. Noah. We'll be by the car." Daniel led them out. He hadn't once talked to Mona. Half the restaurant watched them go.

Noah couldn't help his smile. "See you when I get back?" But he didn't wait for an answer, just slipped on out the door.

This we need most this year . . .

I banished the voice and finished my tally, and Mona and I left Malone's at 3 A.M. Mona was driving, though she was still so pissed she probably shouldn't have been. The city had settled down, and only the homeless were outside, scuffling along sidewalks, huddling in doorways. Mona kept up the chatter she'd started as soon as the boys had left. I didn't know if she was trying to distract me or herself.

"Want to go by and see what's up?" I asked as we got close to home.

"That's the last thing I want to do," she said. "I have the feeling I already know."

"Maybe he was just tired."

"Yeah, maybe." I could tell she didn't believe it. I knew I

should try to comfort her, but I was too busy trying to convince myself that New Year's was just another night. So far it wasn't working. She babbled on about how she should have known better and this kind of stuff always happened to her.

"Stop, hold up," I interrupted her. "Park there."

"Why?" she asked, but pulled alongside the curb. "We're half a block away."

"Just park. And shhh, okay?" I grabbed the huge fruit basket and balloon bouquet Sal had shoved at us as we were leaving and hopped out of the car.

"Samantha!" Mona whispered. "Have you gone completely wack?"

"Shhh," I said. In the doorway near the car, my old woman snored, covered with a ratty old blanket, her two carts wedged around her for protection. A ragged stuffed dog was cradled in her arms. I tied the balloons to the basket, then dug out my tip dollars and tucked them inside. I glanced back to see Mona standing by the car, a *what-are-you-crazy?* look on her face. Moving like a cat, I set the entire thing behind the tallest cart. Then I nodded, patted it quietly—three times on the top and twice on the side—and smiled.

"Happy New Year, Lady," I whispered.

Mona

Thanks to his "friends" from LA, Noah got an agent. The kind he wanted, the kind that could get you commercials and TV auditions as well as modeling gigs. She had him sign up for a television commercial class and get new head shots. Then she sent him for an interview with a manager. Who also signed him. He had to get a second cell phone just for business, and be ready to drop everything to make an audition. Which meant Samantha barely saw him.

"I like him, Mona, but I'm not in love with him," Samantha explained again. "So when he comes over, fine, and when he doesn't—that's okay, too. He's doing what he wants to do, you know?"

Try as I did, I couldn't be like that. When Daniel didn't call, and didn't call, *and didn't call*—I got really depressed.

"Call *him*," Samantha counseled, as we sat together one night with popcorn and TV.

"No."

"Why not?"

"Because that's what I always do. And it never works."

"I thought you weren't in love." She said it gently, but her look said she had never believed it.

"You're right. I don't know. Maybe I am."

"Want me to ask Noah?"

"I already did. He says Daniel's just going through a stage. Nothing's really wrong." I snorted. "Hello. Like I believe him?"

Daniel finally did call, to see if he could stop by.

"See?" Samantha mouthed, when she heard me on the phone.

But the second he walked in the door, I knew it wasn't going to be good. You don't live your entire life with a manic-depressive without getting a sense about people.

"I've been doing a lot of thinking about us," he started.

My stomach twisted. "And?"

"I think maybe we should just, you know . . . take some time off."

My heart seemed to double its beat. "What does that mean?"

"Well, I need time to think about stuff."

"Like what?"

"I don't know, stuff."

I nodded. "Like that girl at your house?"

"What are you talking about?"

"That day you were sick. Someone was there with you."

The little pinpoints of red on his cheeks were enough. "Look, I don't wanna be the bad guy, but I'm not Ryan, okay? I'm not looking for commitment." He sighed. "I never said I was, Mona. You know that."

I nodded. I didn't trust myself to speak just then; there was this huge lump rising in my throat and the back of my eyes was burning. I kept seeing the girl with the holes in her face.

He smiled and touched my arm briefly. I moved away. "So, I guess this is it. You know, for now."

"Yeah, I guess it is."

I tried to do what Samantha did and keep it to myself—but I couldn't. Practically the second she came in that night, the story started pouring out and I couldn't stop it—or the tears. She just wrapped her arms around me and kept saying everything I needed to hear.

"He's a prick, Mona. Face it. And stupid. Can't he see how beautiful you are?"

"Yeah, right."

"Yeah, *right*. You are beautiful and smart and funny and he doesn't even deserve you."

Finally, the tears wore out. I took a big deep breath and blew my nose. "Okay. Now what?" I asked.

"Um, penile mutilation?" She grinned so maliciously I couldn't help but smile.

"Yeah—could I do it?"

"Sure, I'll hold him down."

Now it was me that didn't sleep. And it wasn't *just* because Daniel left. Getting dumped was becoming the story of my life. I didn't have "relationships"—I had "sleeping arrangements," who left when they got tired of hanging out. You have to be some kind of *big-time* loser to put up with that. I didn't say anything to Samantha about it, or even to Erica, in our morning carpool therapy sessions. For them, I pretended I was getting a little better each day.

"Okay. Good façade you've been putting on," Erica said one morning. "But he's really not worth it."

"Stop beating yourself up," Samantha said that same day, later. "This is *not* your fault. It wasn't you."

But in those 3 A.M. conversations with myself, I figured something out. It *was* me. No one else made my choices, and I was the only one who could make myself okay. I just didn't know how to do it.

"From my mom?" Samantha asked, taking the UPS package I pointed to as she came through the door. I loved getting presents, even if they weren't actually mine.

"Who else?" I asked, starting to rip it open for her.

"I'll do it. Just let me take off my coat."

"See what happens when you don't call her back?"

"It's probably more sheets," she said, and tore off the brown packing tape. Inside was a large, beat-up canvas bag. "Oh great. My dance bag," she muttered, throwing out what I called her Duh-Sammie look. She held up her index finger. "But wait—do I dance anymore? No. So why would I need this, hm? What the hell is wrong with her?"

She tossed it over to the couch and half the stuff spilled out. I helped her pick up shoes and tights. "Mm, smells yummy," I said, and she made a face at me. Left on the floor was a newspaper. On the inside front page, clearly outlined by a thick red marker, was the picture of a dark-haired girl, arms raised, in the middle of a dance step.

Samantha took a quick sharp breath when she saw it. I reached over to grab it up.

"Oh shit," I blurted. "Is that . . .?"

"Yeah. And me," she said, pointing to the hand in the corner, with the body cut off.

"God, she was beautiful," I ventured, handing the paper to Samantha.

"Yeah, well. I guess she was, huh."

"But you're right, I don't look like her at all." That got a little smile. "What does the article say?" I asked.

"My old dance company's having a concert." She gave the paper back. "Here. You read."

"Wow. They're giving an award in her name," I said.

"You can say Julie. It's okay," Samantha said.

"Sorry."

"Yeah. It's not an award, it's a scholarship. For dance." Samantha was up now, pacing. "The show's a fund-raiser. We did a whole bunch when we were trying to get money for the company to tour LA. You can make tons."

"I'll go with you, if you want."

"No, that's all right."

"You're going by yourself?" I asked.

"I'm not going at all."

"Samantha, are you sure? I mean, it's a great chance—"

"Mona . . . stop. Please."

"I'm sorry, but don't you think—"

"Look, you didn't know Jules, so how would you know, huh? But this is the worst. All these people making a big deal out of her." She shook her head. "She would have hated it."

"Do you think maybe they just want to, you know . . . honor her?"

"Maybe they should have thought of that before she died."

I opened my mouth to say something else, then shut it again. Samantha's face softened. "I'm sorry. I'm always yelling at you about this, and it isn't you at all, is it?"

"It's okay."

"Hey. I forgot to tell you. I saw Daniel today. He asked about you."

"Stop. You're just changing the subject."

"No, really, he was with Noah and they stopped by Malone's."

"You swear?"

"I swear. He wanted to know if you were seeing anybody."

"And? What did you say?"

"I said yes, of course."

"Why did you do that? What if he wants to come over or something?"

"You'll say no."

I sighed.

"Won't you?"

I sighed again.

"Mona . . . "

"Okay, okay, I'll say no."

"You see? And everybody told me you couldn't be taught."

Samantha

The Belrose was lit the way it always was for performances, and cars lined both sides of the street. A banner hung prominently outside: THE JULIANA MICHAELS SCHOLARSHIP CONCERT. I got there minutes before curtain, parked down a couple blocks, and sat in my Jeep. Twice I started it up, and twice I turned it off again. This felt entirely too familiar.

> *"Hurry up!" Jules snarls and snatches her dance bag from the back of my car, calling over her shoulder, "I told you we shouldn't have stopped for gas!"*

With a sigh, I propelled myself up and out of the car. I marched toward the front door, knowing if I hesitated, I would turn around and go home. The woman at the box office wasn't anyone I recognized. I pulled out my fifteen dollars and handed it to her, even managing to smile.

> *"One minute to places," the stage manager calls.*
> *Jules and I duck in the alcove at the back of the dressing*

room and hold hands, locking fingers, staring deep. This time she nods first.

"Places!"

With a high-five, we're on our way.

"There's a seat in the back, over there. But please, dear, they're starting," she warned, a finger to her lips. "Try to be quiet."

"Quiet backstage," the stage manager whispers, and I find Jules in the opposite wing. We breathe and focus front, then mouth the last count before our cue: a-five-six-seven-eight. . . .

Just as the house lights dimmed, I spotted Linda, in her usual seat by the left side of the audience. The curtains began to slowly open, and I heard the low opening notes of the number we'd used last season to start the show. The outlines of the dancers began to appear behind the scrim. My eyes went to where Jules and I would have been, and my heart started to beat faster, just like it always did. Except I wasn't on that stage now, and I never would be again. Jules had been the reason I danced, and Jules was . . .

Suddenly, I couldn't quite catch my breath. There didn't seem to be enough air. I bumped into the man sitting next to me and couldn't manage a "sorry." I just had to get out.

"Are you all right?" the box office lady asked, as I brushed past her, but I didn't answer, just pushed open the door she was guarding and hurried out. I gulped in a lungful of air; it didn't help. I needed to get to my Jeep. Lightheaded now, I jumped in and turned it on—then stopped. I was trembling all over; I felt like I could pass out. If I drove, I'd kill myself. I shook my head to clear it and took another deep breath.

This was stupid. Why was I even here? I hadn't intended to come; not once since I got the invitation did I think it would be a good idea. But then last night, my Lady had banged lightly on the trash can below the window. She'd waited for me to look out and see her. Then she'd grinned, but not in the usual way, with her hand covering her mouth. This time, it was real, and her eyes had sparkled, and I'd seen the spaces where her teeth were missing. Even so, she'd looked like a little girl. Shyly, she held up a tiny bunch of dandelions, tied together with a ribbon. She pointed up at me and blew a kiss on a finger, nodded a couple of times, and gently placed the flowers on the top of the can. With one last nod, she grabbed her carts and trundled off. And I'd sat there and I'd cried. Just like the night at Malone's with the song; the tears came on their own. She was trying to connect with me. And suddenly I'd understood that I needed to connect to someone, too.

Except this wasn't right. This wasn't where it was going to happen. The show might be "for" Jules—but she wasn't in it, she wouldn't have liked it, and there was no way I could stay. I took another deep breath. I was calmer now, I could head home. Except I never made it past Jules's freeway exit, because all of a sudden, I knew exactly where I was supposed to go.

"Listen, Sam, can't you hear it talking?"

"You're crazy, you know that? It's an ocean."

"Yes, but it's my ocean. It talks. Shhh. Listen. Can't you hear it?"

Just past Jules's street was the road that led out to Stinson Beach.

How different it was alone. The farther I got from town, the more I felt that I'd left the real world and was on a road that wouldn't ever end. I rounded a turn, and the moon dipped behind a canopy of trees. I felt like I did driving home from the hotel—like the old lady must have, the night she'd caught me in the window. Someone or something was watching me—some kind of scary "presence." I started to panic again, and made myself slow down for the last big curve, where you finally see the ocean below you. When it came into view, the fear went away.

This was right. This was where I needed to be. The moon cast a glow on the water and the sand, and I smiled as I got out of the car.

Two little boys tossed a ball back and forth. An older couple huddled together close to the water, the man draping his arm around the woman. I pulled my parka around me and strolled along the shore until I found a nook in the rocks I could tuck myself into. It wouldn't be warm, but I'd be out of the wind. A woman called out, and the boys went complaining into a yard. A dog barked briefly and was shushed. The only sound left was the waves gently lapping on the sand. The ocean was "talking."

Hunkering down, I stared up at the sky and took a long, slow breath, savoring the salt air. The stars were startling in their brightness. But it all made sense, and as long as I was here—so did I. I could relax. I didn't have to think, explain, or figure anything out. I could listen to the ocean and stare at the sky and breathe the air—and be okay. Not great, not happy . . . but okay.

A year and a half ago, Jules and I had sat right here, in this exact place. A year and a half ago, she'd cried about losing Jack to Rachael. I'd told her she was stupid for loving him, and she'd turned those Scorpio eyes in my direction and I'd been so very afraid she might choose him over me. *A year and a half ago!* When there was no such thing as cancer. I was just Sam and she was my One and Only. We danced. And we couldn't ever die.

With a sigh, I stood and brushed off the sand. The lights in the beach houses were gone. The older couple had disappeared. I walked down the beach, like we had then, smiling a little as I remembered how we'd danced every time the waves lapped over our toes. A cloud passed in front of the moon, snuffing the light, and once again I felt like the old homeless lady. I jerked my head around to one side, then the other, to see who was watching me.

"Just go back to the car," I said out loud. But instead of calmly walking back, I started to jog. When another shadow crossed me, I broke into a run. I tried to argue with the panic, but it wasn't working. Something was out to get me. Something I couldn't see. I ran harder, until I couldn't hear the ocean, and the mountains disappeared. I rounded the bluff with my heart pounding. I couldn't feel my legs, but I kept running until a sharp rip in my side sent me sprawling. And there I stuck, on my hands and knees, gulping air.

Stupid girl—stupid, stupid girl. No one was watching, nothing would "get" me. I was one hundred percent completely alone out here. The mountain stood placidly behind me; the moon shimmered in the sky and on the water; the ocean calmly slapped down on the beach. Everything was exactly as it should be. I sat back and looked around. A seagull appeared out of nowhere, startling me. It perched on a tiny mound of sand barely ten feet away.

"Somebody chasing you, too, huh?" I said to the bird. It tilted its head, no doubt wondering what this big person was doing out here in the middle of the night. It poked a bit in the sand and considered me again. I waved my arm and it flew off. Then I sighed. I should've left it alone—at least it was company. I looked out over the water—the ocean was so different when it was dark. One little tear found its way out of my eye, and down my cheek. Another followed. They plopped softly on the sand.

"Oh my Jules," I whispered to the night, "I miss you."

My tears fell a little faster, and all of a sudden, I felt the watcher again, dark and scary and close. But I had no more energy for running, and besides, nothing could possibly hurt me more than I was hurting already. A low moaning sound started, and it took me a minute to realize it was coming from me. The tears broke loose completely, and I sobbed like that early morning in the hospital. Endlessly. There didn't seem to be a way to stop. Because I would never ever hear her voice again or see her laughing or watch how she held her back so tall when she danced. Because Jules was gone. And she would never ever come back.

The moon sat in a different part of the sky and the entire horizon had nestled down under a blanket of thick, white fog. I found myself curled in a little ball, my head tucked inside my arms. I must have cried myself to sleep. Ever so slowly, I unwound, brushing the sand from the side of my face. My parka was soaked from the foggy air. I shivered, cold to my very bones.

My hips and back were stiff, my nose was stuffed, waves lapped peacefully on the shore. At least the awful pain had subsided. Except the empty feeling I had now was just as bad.

And the seagull was back. Staring.

"What's your problem, bird?" I said out loud, my voice cracked and hoarse. I sounded like Sal. "You lonely, too, huh?" The gull cocked its head to one side and didn't waver a bit in its gaze.

Suddenly, I could see Jules and me at Brooke's house on the ocean, and how we watched the seagulls "dancing." One of them had come right inside and stared up at her. I smiled, remembering how she'd loved that. Then I shook my head and stretched, and brushed myself off. That was then, and this was now. It was time to move on. Time to get home. Mona would be frantic, wondering where I was.

The bird poked around in the sand, came up with some tidbit and swallowed it. Then it turned and hopped right up toward me, not two feet away, and stared at me again. And stared. And stared.

I flung my arm out and the gull jumped a little, flapped its wings a few times and then settled back down in the sand, just a tad closer. Its head tilted one way, then the other, and it took a few more tentative steps in my direction.

"I'm warning you, bird . . . " I said, even louder, and flung my arms once more. This time it stuck its chest out and didn't budge. Not one inch. My heart did a funny little bounce. The gull tilted its head one more time—and winked. I froze, mouth slightly open, eyes unblinking. I could hear my breath in my throat, and I knew I was believing what I didn't have any reason to believe.

This was no seagull, it was Jules. Like the wisp of a breeze, an eyelash tickling—she was here.

Suddenly, I understood the watcher and the danger, and I knew that it would never fully leave me; it was the hole in the world where Jules used to be. I started crying again; but these tears connected to something inside me that connected me back to life, and to Jules. I gazed up at the bird and nodded once. She stared and nodded back and with one more little wink, flew away.

And Jules was gone, once again.

Part
THREE

~

"Trouble is, son, the farther you run,
the more you feel undefined. . . . "

Samantha

I sit by Jules's bed and watch her face and stroke her arm and listen to her breathing. Sometimes it almost stops and I hold my breath, too. Sometimes her hand shoots up in the air and thumps back down to her body. Once her lips quiver, like she's thinking of something sad and wants to tell me, but of course she can't talk anymore.

Never in my life have I been so utterly and completely present. I can smell Sandra's fear, see the dread in William's face. I'm connected to each and every moment, conscious of my breathing, the sound of my heart, the exact blending of colors in the hospital room, how the tiles in the corner by the bathroom are not evenly set.

I didn't want to remember this.

I know I arrived late in the morning, which changed to afternoon, and then night, but I have no sense of it inside the hospital—everything is fluorescent. Somehow this room exists without time, and even as I know we are racing toward the impossible, the minutes stand still. Or maybe we're standing outside of them.

Friends and family come to visit, wearing faces that don't quite belong to them. They talk to Sandra and me in voices I can't recognize and go in to look at Jules, but I don't think they really see her. Nurses adjust things, but there are no more tubes now, just machines sitting useless and unimportant. The oncologist, Dr. Conner, hovers along the edges, looking pissed but doing nothing. No one stays too long. Just Sandra and William and me.

And Jules, of course—tiny and scarred—hair struggling to grow back once again, needle tracks from all the IVs, muscles wasted, a red slash near her throat that used to be the shunt for chemo. I want her back like she used to be—laughing and dancing, not frozen and quiet and pale, so skinny that her bones practically stick through her skin. I run my hand down her arm and then stop. Her hands are still hers; unchanged. Long perfect fingers, delicate dancer hands. I smile. Sandra has painted her nails baby pink.

"You have to tell her good-bye," Sandra whispers. "She waited for you. She can't leave until you let her go."

How can I let her go? But—oh God—how can I possibly want her to stay here like this—so very still, with no music? I stroke her face, then lean over and kiss her. I smooth the short hair back and hold her hand to my cheek.

"Good-bye, my dancer, my friend, my One and Only. I love you."

The image was too strong. I was there again. Seeing it. Feeling it.

Two hours later, Sandra's alone with her. She's just washed her face and is using a hankie to dab water on her lips. Jules's lips are really dry. The skin on her chest and arms looks almost transparent now. I can hardly hear her breathing. I gently stroke her arm, up and down, like I did when I'd first come, but this time she doesn't respond.

Her body feels different, harder, heavy against the air. I stare at her face. Something has changed.

"Go get some rest, sweetie," Sandra says in her mom voice. When I don't move or answer, she slips an arm around me and leads me to the door. "I'll be here. I'll call you." I walk to the waiting room and curl up in a light green armchair, across from William.

My heart turned in my chest, warning me. Get up, it said. Get dressed for work. Go out to Mona. Call your mom. Take a walk. Visit Noah. Take a drive. Do something. But it was no use. There was no halfway anymore. And no hiding.

Sandra touches me lightly on the shoulder and suddenly I'm breathing fast. In the same instant that I stand there in the waiting room, I float off into some other dimension, watching. I don't move an inch, but inside I'm falling, screaming without sound, like in dreams. I try to concentrate so I can figure out what to do, but something's squeezing my brain, something cold and dark and scarier than I can think of. Sandra's face is very clear . . .

And I know.

I just can't make the words, even in my mind. She has to say them for me.

"She's gone, Sammie."

Mona

"Toilet paper?"

"Oh, shit, I forgot."

"Samantha!"

"I'm sorry, I'll go get it now."

"No, I'll go. You eat some dinner." I grabbed a jacket from my room and scooped up my keys. She smiled apologetically—it was the second time this week she'd promised and then forgotten to bring something home. She was still in her Malone's "uniform" and I couldn't help noticing how the pants—which used to be skin tight—now bagged in her butt. "You're getting too damn skinny," I told her.

"Yeah, I know."

"Go eat. I made spaghetti. It actually tastes pretty good."

"Mona . . . "

"Yeah?"

"I'm really sorry."

Sometime around February, Julie had moved in with us. She lived in Samantha's eyes and took up all the space that used to belong to me and Noah. I couldn't say exactly when I noticed it and I sure as hell didn't know why *now*, all of a sudden. But there it was. She still didn't sleep that good. But now, she *did* cry—in her room, at dinner, sitting watching TV—you name it. She probably cried all the way to work. And she told me more than I really wanted to know about "Jules."

Be careful what you wish for, huh?

Like a few nights ago. We were on our way home from a long-overdue food shopping. Noah didn't come by as much now, so our take-out connection had dried up, and we were faced with cooking if we wanted to eat. We'd actually had a great time together being silly in the supermarket and now had twelve bags of food in the back of the Jeep. All of a sudden, Samantha pointed to a guy walking his dog.

"Shit, Mona, look! See him? Look at him, check him out."

He was definitely not my idea of good-looking. "I'd stick with Noah, if I were you."

"No no no. *I* don't like him. But shit—he looks exactly like Jack."

"Oh, yeah, wow, that's amazing." I rolled my eyes at her. "Who the hell is Jack?"

"Sorry. Jack was Jules's boyfriend." She slowed down to check him out again. I sighed to myself. So much for hanging out together. "Damn. Exactly like him." She shook her head. "He was a real shit."

"Oh yeah?" I thought immediately of Daniel. "Jules" and I might have something in common after all.

"She got revenge, though." Samantha's eyes had that distant, remembering look. "Big time." She smiled. "She was one crazy girl."

"Really?" I smiled, too, but wasn't feeling it. "What did she do?"

"Well, it was when she first stopped chemo and came back to school, and Jack was over by the theater with Rachael, who was this complete bitch, and there they were, like, groping each other, and she strutted right up to them and . . . oh never mind." Samantha said it with a sigh, dismissing me with a little wave of her hand. "It wouldn't make any sense. You had to know her."

I nodded. "Right." We turned onto our street in silence, but she was smiling, still in the memory, and now her eyes were moist. "Oh—there." I pointed. "Wow, we actually get to park in front."

She pulled in and we grabbed the bags out of the car. "She used to call me Sam, you know," Samantha said on the way up the stairs.

"I figured."

She turned to me, surprised. "You did?"

"Yeah, the day we met. When we went for coffee."

"At that place across the street."

"Mm-hm. And I asked what people called you, and you said most people called you 'Sammie.'"

"Okay, yeah, and . . . ?"

"And I said, *I'm* going to call you 'Sam.' And you turned even whiter than you usually are."

"I did?"

"Yep. I figured there was something, and you didn't want to talk about it. And I figured you probably had billions of friends, and I didn't want to be just another Sammie person. That's why I call you Samantha." I peeked over at her, suddenly wanting to be noticed and acknowledged. But she'd already moved on.

We spent the whole rest of the evening together. As I listened to "Jules and I this" and "Jules and I that," I wondered why the hell I'd wanted these stories in the first place. I couldn't do anything about it. I couldn't really "share" her experience—I hadn't been there. I hadn't even known her while it was happening. And as far as seeing myself hold her when she cried, and knowing the right thing to say—that was entirely stupid. When she cried, she tucked herself into a tiny little ball and didn't want me near. And there wasn't anything anyone could say to help. She wouldn't allow it.

That's what it was. Not that Julie had died. Not even that Samantha was sad now, and remembering, and crying all the time. The thing I couldn't deal with was the wall she'd built to hide behind. Maybe it had been there all along, but I was really conscious of it now. She'd disappeared almost completely. The only one allowed inside was Jules. I might be in the room with her, but I could have been anyone.

That night, I waited until she turned out her light, then dialed Noah's cell. He was the only person I knew who might understand what I was feeling, because he'd been feeling it, too. He answered after just one ring.

"Hey, it's Mona."

"Hey."

"Where are you right now? Can you talk?"

"To you? Always. What's up?"

"You're not in the middle of something?"

"The shoot's way over. Weather changed."

"Okay, then," I sighed and took a chance. "Tell me I'm a good person."

He chuckled a bit. "You're a great person," he replied.

"So, it's just that *no one* can compare to 'Jules'?"

He full-on laughed. "Basically, yeah. I think that's about it."

"So then, is it really awful that it pisses me off? I mean, I want to *be there* and all that . . . but that's all she talks about now."

"Wait, what happened to 'She'll get over it,' 'Be patient,' and all that bullshit you were telling me?"

"I know, I'm sorry."

"Sucks, doesn't it?"

"Yeah, and I don't know what to do."

"Hang in there. It's got to pass eventually."

"You think?"

"Yeah, I mean, time heals, right? Besides, I'll be home on Saturday. Then you won't be out there all on your own."

Samantha

"Sal? What was it like on the first anniversary, you know, of when Laura died?"

He stopped sorting checks and peered over at me, his face looking more than ever like Doc of the Seven Dwarfs. "That's not your business, is it?"

"I thought maybe you'd tell me anyway."

"Why should I talk to you?"

I fought back my stupid tears. "Because I really need to know?"

He stared hard a second, then looked back down, as if he were making a decision. I knew he was remembering the night he'd found me crying out back. "I got drunk. Shit-faced, falling-down drunk."

"Did it help?"

"Not a bit."

"Oh."

He peered at me again. "Sammie, it's not the same for us. Laura was my wife for twenty-nine years."

I glared back. "And Jules was my best friend. For more than half my life."

Sal sighed, then deliberately turned away from me. A second later, he stood and put the checks away in the drawer. "We should go down. It's about time."

"We've got another half an hour."

"We'll go anyway."

I filed the invoices and followed him down to the restaurant. His shoulders were hunched up and he didn't make eye contact with me at all as he gave out the floor assignments. As usual these days, I had to work doubly hard to keep track of everything I was supposed to do. And, as usual, I was exhausted by the time I got to my first break. Sal found me in the back with Chloe, having tea. He waved her away.

"Okay," he announced, drawing a stool up close to where I sat. "You got a question? Ask. Don't expect great answers."

All of a sudden, I didn't know what to say. "I guess . . . I guess it's just one thing. I don't know . . . it sounds stupid, but do you ever get to be yourself again?"

He sighed and turned away, looking down at his foot for a minute. Then he stared directly into my eyes. "No." He shook his head. "No, Sammie, I don't think you ever do."

The Jeep was now my favorite place to cry. My eyes went to the other seat, Jules's seat. I imagined her kicked back, feet up on the dash, chocolate eyes flashing, and off I went. Since it was raining *outside*, too, I focused extra hard on seeing the stoplights and watching for pedestrians. This was getting ridiculous. I had to laugh at myself. I needed Jules here to tell me what to do.

My storm subsided by the time I got home, but the rain outside was worse, so of course there was no parking. I made all the routine circles on the surrounding streets—still nothing. I had to widen the circle to the warehouse district, and sure enough, the whole block was empty. I parked as close as I could to our street, making sure there weren't any people lurking in the shadows. This was not a good neighborhood to be alone in at night.

Suddenly—déjà vu. Three weeks after my dad had given me the Jeep, Jules and I had gone into San Francisco. We weren't supposed to—one of the rules my mom made when she agreed to the car was that I wouldn't cross any bridges—but Jules had seen an article on a ballet master from Russia who was opening a studio. His name was Dmitri Volovochev and he was giving a free master class. And the studio was on this street.

I think I must have known that when we moved into the apartment. But I wasn't thinking about Jules then, or dancing, so I guess I'd filed it away somewhere. So now the déjà vu hit hard. I'd been scared to leave my Jeep then, too. Jules, of course, had bounced out the minute we stopped. Dressed in a pair of short shorts over her black leotard and pink tights, her hair in a tight little bun, her dance bag over her shoulder, she even smiled at the surly homeless guy who wanted money. She was going to dance. Nothing could get in her way.

I was jealous that day. A lot. Because Jules absolutely knew what she wanted in her life. And all I knew for sure was that I was friends with Jules. Then it turned out the class was too hard for me, so I sneaked out the side door. Several other girls and boys had dropped out, too. I stood where I wouldn't be obvious, feeling less than human, and watched Jules work.

She was sweating; tiny beads dripped down the sides of her face, and her leotard was drenched. Sometime in the middle of the *adage*, the teacher focused on her. He stood right behind her with his cane and poked at her as she concentrated on performing.

"You do again," he said, spitting out the words in his thick Russian accent. "Again" and "again" and "again."

Nothing was good enough; he barked and rapped his cane on the floor and made corrections on things no one else would even notice. He never stopped. For the rest of the class, he wouldn't leave her alone. Jules just gritted her teeth and worked harder. As they went across the floor, she leapt higher than ever, and her turns were the most precise. He screamed at her during the combination, and she was brilliant. After class, he called her over. I watched carefully, but couldn't tell if he was making her laugh or cry. I waited by the door, and we didn't even speak until we had pulled away and were almost to the bridge.

"So that sucked, huh?" I ventured. She looked over at me like I was speaking Swedish or something. "The way he was picking on you," I explained.

"He was correcting me, Sam."

"He was harassing you, Jules."

"Whatever. I loved it."

"You're crazy." I was glad I was driving. Her face was too bright.

"Do you know what he said?" she asked, and touched my arm. "He called me a *dancer*."

"So what? I call you a dancer all the time."

"Yeah, but you're my best friend. You're supposed to. Volovochev is like . . . I don't know. God."

Mona

"You are wearing a hole in our floor," I insisted, smiling, as I watched Noah track from the living room down the hall and back to the kitchen. "Sit down, will you? Relax. She'll be here."

"Let's just you and me go, okay?" he asked for the millionth time.

"Come on, you know you want to tell Samantha."

"I really don't."

"Noah!"

"Shit, I barely see her anymore."

"Because you're always busy."

He wagged a finger at me. "Not exactly the whole story there, Mon."

"I know, I know. But be honest, huh? Don't you want to tell her? Just a little bit?"

"Yeah, maybe I do." He gave me that amazing model smile, and I felt that familiar thrill. "But I want to tell her *now*."

"You're such a big old kid." Just then, the doorbell rang in the two short bursts we used to signal each other. "See. There she is!"

Pushing his shoulders back like he was getting ready for

war, Noah opened the door. A very wet Samantha traipsed up the stairs.

"No parking," I said.

"Of course not," she answered. "Too much rain."

"Guess what?" Noah said.

"Okay, but could I come in first?"

"Oh, sure, yeah, come on in." Noah grimaced a little.

"Maybe she could even take off those wet clothes?" I suggested. I gently pushed her toward her room, as Noah parked himself on the back of the couch and made a face at me. A second later, she was back, in a dry shirt, toweling off her hair. I noticed she'd trimmed it again and wondered when she'd done it.

"Okay—what?" She asked as she came back out, looking from him to me and back again.

"Guess," Noah insisted, grinning like the Cheshire Cat.

"You won the lottery?"

"Better."

"Um, you inherited a million dollars?"

"Almost. I got a commercial! No, I'm sorry. Not one commercial. A whole series of them—for Nike. Sammie, they're going to be based *on me!* They want to do someone who's not famous—and I'm it! Do you understand what I'm saying? I am going to be the main guy in all those nationwide Nike commercials!" He was electrified.

"Really?" She looked at me for confirmation.

"He found out this afternoon," I explained, nodding. "They're flying him to New York in April. He's filming for at least two weeks."

"Whoa—Noah! Congratulations!"

"This is not scale, either," Noah continued. "My agent *nego-tiated*. Do you know how rich I'm going to be?"

"Noah, you're already rich," Samantha reminded him.

"No, no, no—my *mother* is rich. My *father* is rich. I am a starving artist who lives in a loft."

"Okay, okay. Got it," she said.

"Now, I will be a successful starving artist."

"You'll probably still be a jerk, though, don't you think?" I asked, and grinned at Samantha.

"Yeah, but then I can afford it." He grabbed Samantha's hand. "Come on, we're going over to my place to celebrate."

She pulled back. "Now?"

"Yes, now. What did you think?"

"It's after eleven o'clock."

"So? Come on! Ryan's got a bunch of people waiting."

"What about Daniel?" Samantha asked me.

"No problem," I said. "Daniel's at his new girlfriend's house, but what the fuck, huh?"

"Shit, Mona. When did that happen? Why didn't you say something?"

"Actually, I did. When I saw him with her? But it doesn't matter, because, read my lips—I *really* don't care." I managed a pretty reasonable smile. "So, shall we go party?"

Samantha turned back to Noah. "I don't know, Noah. I mean, it's really incredible, I'm totally psyched for you, but I'm exhausted. Could we maybe do something tomorrow night instead?"

He shot me a "told you so" look and then smiled at

Samantha. His voice stayed deceptively mellow. "Why? You depressed?"

"No, like I said, I'm tired, and—"

"'Cause that shit's getting a little old, you know?"

"Noah, stop," I warned.

"I'm not depressed, Noah," Samantha said.

"Right. Your eyes are just red from the pollution? Never mind, it doesn't matter. Whatever."

"Come on, man," I said. "She's tired. She's been working."

"*I'm* tired," he argued back. "I've been working, too."

"Fine," Samantha said. "I'll change."

"Don't do me any favors, huh?"

"I said I'll change."

"Look, let's just forget it, okay?" He glanced at me. "Mona, you still coming?" Before I could answer, he glared at Samantha. "Why don't you stay here and cry or something, huh? You'll have more fun."

"God, you're a shit," Samantha said, in a low voice.

"Am I?" He shook his head. "Check again. You're the one who spends all her time thinking about dead people. 'Cause—news flash—the girl *is* dead."

"Noah!" I said.

"No, it's time somebody said it." He put on his coat. "There's other people here, Sammie, and we're still alive. You might try paying attention to us once in a while."

He walked out, leaving the door open behind him. Samantha stared after him. I closed it quietly.

"I'm sorry, Samantha. That sucked."

"Is that how you feel, too?"

"No, no, it isn't. Not at all."

"Because I can't help what's going on with me, Mona."

"I know."

"Do you?"

I sighed, waited a second, then spoke again. "Yeah. You're having a hard time."

"Wow, really?"

I ignored her sarcasm. "Do you think it might help to talk to somebody? There's grief counselors, you know, or I could call my mom's doctor . . . " She whipped her head in my direction, and I'd swear I'd seen that expression on my mother's face. Like she could slap me and not even care.

"I thought you were going to the party." She marched into the kitchen and opened the refrigerator door.

"I don't need to. I'll stay with you."

"What good will that do?" She snatched the milk out and slammed the door. "I mean, what if I get *depressed* and *cry*?"

"That's not fair, Samantha."

"Yeah, well, that's life, huh?"

"Look, if you want—"

"Right now, I just want you to leave me alone, Mona. Do you think you could?"

I waited a second before speaking. She was upset and this time, I *wasn't* going to leave her alone. She needed me. "Samantha, come on. Please? We're best friends, remember?"

"Are we?"

"Aren't we?"

She caught me with a stare that went straight through my eyes and sliced into my heart. "My best friend is dead."

I caught up to Noah as he crossed the street. I couldn't fix things with anybody, not Daniel, not my mom, and certainly not Samantha. I would never be the kind of friend she needed me to be—it wasn't a human possibility.

Noah saw the tears and wrapped both his arms around me. He pulled me close and held me, right in the middle of the sidewalk. I felt him sigh and realized he didn't know what to do, either. Then he took my hand and, without looking back, we headed for his apartment.

Samantha

The dance bag perched on the corner of my bed, stuffed with my jazz and ballet shoes, pointe shoes, and all the warmups and leotards I'd been taking on the tour. Through the rip in the top near where the zipper closed, I could see the blue of Jules's favorite T-shirt. She'd given it to me the night of the tour "kick-off" banquet, insisting it would bring me "stuff," our word for luck—which of course you can never say right out loud. I smiled, remembering all our superstitions about shows, then sighed as the memory invited tears.

Mona wasn't home yet. Three in the morning, and sleep was not happening. I'd cleaned up the kitchen and thrown out everything that smelled bad in the refrigerator, which was most of it. At two, I'd called Noah's, but the machine picked up. I'd thought about walking over, but what would I say? I realized I was pacing, exactly the way my mom used to do when my dad wasn't coming home, so I peeked once out the window and then plopped down on the bed. Not even my old lady was around.

The dance bag glared at me. That was a stupid idea, too; I didn't know why I had dragged it out of my closet. I wouldn't

take a dance class, not even at the studio only blocks away. I
snorted at that thought. Especially not there. I shoved the bag
onto the floor and lay back on my pillow.

Like dominoes, one thought I didn't want triggered the next
and the next, until I felt like I would explode. Mona got all
mixed up with Jules, and everything I'd ever done that was stupid or selfish paraded itself through my brain. I thought of the
times I'd lied to my mom and my dad, and awful things I'd done
to teachers or Brooke or Sarah. It was out of control. No logic
anywhere; I was trapped in a whirlwind of Sammie-mistakes
and I didn't know how to get free. With a sigh, I rolled out of
bed and went in for the phone. I hadn't talked to Sandra since
before we moved out. But I had no one else I could call.

"Hello?" Sandra's voice was sleepy. I almost hung up.

"Hi."

"Sammie?" She perked up immediately, just like she always
had. "Oh, Sammie, it's good to hear your voice." She paused. I
could almost see her expression. "You okay, sweetie?"

"Yeah. I guess. I can't sleep. I'm sorry I woke you."

"Don't worry about it."

"This is so weird. I mean, we haven't even talked."

"Not important. Are you sure you're okay?"

"Yeah. No. Shit, I don't know."

"Tell me, sweetie. What happened? What's going on?"

"Nothing really, I guess. I don't know. My boyfriend was having this party, and I didn't want to go and he said all kinds of
awful things and I got pissed at the girl I live with, her name is
Mona . . . instead of him and she went and it's all just so . . . "

"Fucked up?"

I laughed right out loud, in surprise. I'd never heard her use that expression. "Yeah. That's exactly what it is."

"Everything feels upside down?"

"Yeah."

"Like you're totally out of control."

"Exactly."

Her voice was incredibly gentle. "You know what it is, sweetie—you're missing Julie."

I paused a second before answering. She could always go right to the truth. "Yeah. I am. A lot."

She sighed. "This sadness . . . it's very long, isn't it?"

"It sure is." I sighed, too, and started to tear up. "I'm really stupid these days, I can't stop crying." Then I started to laugh. "Listen to me! Do you think I'm going crazy?"

Sandra chuckled along with me. "Oh no, that'd be far too easy." She was quiet a second, then spoke in that same soft tone. "You have to try to find her, Sammie."

"I have. It doesn't work."

"Think of stuff you did with her, things she said . . ."

"Doesn't help. I just cry more." I remembered the seagull. "Besides, what difference does it make? She's gone."

"I'm sorry. I don't believe that."

"Well, she is."

"No, Sammie. She can't be. She did things, she loved people . . . she danced. All that energy has to be somewhere."

"How do *you* know?"

"Well, I don't."

"Then why do you keep saying to find her?" Without meaning to, I sounded angry.

Sandra sighed and I could hear the tears in her voice this time. "Because I don't know what else to do."

Of course she couldn't see it, but I nodded. We were both quiet for a second, then I blurted, "I hate that she died. I hate feeling like this. I want it to be over."

Sandra took a long deep breath. "I don't know for sure, Sammie, but I think maybe it never is. I think maybe we have to learn to live around it."

I nodded again and cried almost silently. Sandra waited a moment before she spoke. "I'd love to see you."

"Me, too."

"It's coming up, you know?"

"Yeah."

"Maybe we can get together before then."

"All right."

"Are you okay to go to sleep now?"

"I think so."

"I love you."

"I love you, too."

When I woke up the next morning, Mona still wasn't home. The lights were on in the living room, and her bed hadn't been slept in. I made coffee and plopped myself down on the couch, trying to imagine what I could possibly say to make things better. Maybe if I went by her work, took her out to lunch . . . I could offer to loan her that shirt of my mine she always liked, or . . . suddenly I froze, remembering.

* * *

"Take this," Jules whispers as she hands me the T-shirt at the ban-quet. Inside is something hard. I unwrap a cassette tape that's marked, "For Sam Only." She touches my arm. "Listen to it later."

"I want to listen now."

"No." She has trouble getting the words to come out with enough sound so I can hear them. "Later. Promise?"

"Okay."

"Promise promise?*"*

"Promise promise."

I shivered. This was what Sandra meant. I raced to my room, threw myself across the bed and grabbed the dance bag. I yanked out the shirt. The tape was still there, wrapped up; I could see myself packing it. I walked into the living room and kneeled by the tape deck. Carefully, because my hands were shaking really badly, I slid the tape in, sat back and pushed "play."

"Hey Sam, it's me . . ."

It was her real voice, the one she had before the cancer made it raspy and tired. My arm shot forward before my brain had time to react. I slammed the "eject" button so hard, the tape flew out and the entire unit slipped off the back edge of the shelf. I felt like somebody had punched me in the stomach. I snatched up the tape, and shoved it and the shirt back in the dance bag.

Not now, Jules. I'm sorry. Not yet.

Mona

Mom sat stiffly on a chair in the corner of her room, no make-up, with her hair in a French braid. She could've been my older sister instead of my mother. We stared at each other as Aunt Mollye bustled about, pulling up covers and straightening things, chattering as she worked.

My mother had had an "episode." The police had found her wandering in the Marin City Shopping Center at four in the morning, muttering that someone had stolen her child. Aunt Mollye's name was in her wallet, so now she was back at Marin General, in the psychiatric ward, getting her meds straightened out and doing intensive therapy. It certainly wasn't the first time, and it probably wouldn't be the last. Once again, I promised myself that if I ever got this disease, I wouldn't let it take control.

Mom spoke first. "She wasn't supposed to call you."

"Well, she did. And here I am."

"You weren't supposed to call her, Mollye."

"She's your *daughter*, for goodness' sake," Aunt Mollye said. Mom got that petulant look and drew her robe closer around her body. "No. My daughter would keep me from wandering about making a damn fool of myself."

"You want me to go, Mom?" I asked. Mollye froze in the middle of plumping a pillow, and turned her face toward me. The tone of my voice had surprised all of us, none more than me. I sounded strong. And separate.

"What?" my mom asked.

"Do you want me to go?"

"Do what you want."

"No. It's your room. *You* tell *me*. Do you want me to stay or do you want me to go?"

Mollye finished the first pillow and picked up the other one. When Mom looked over at her, she didn't return the glance.

"Go," Mom said.

"Fine. Good-bye." I turned toward the door. "See ya, Aunt Mollye."

"No. Stay." Mom whispered it.

"What? I couldn't hear you."

Mom cleared her throat. "I said, I want you to stay."

I stood frozen in the doorway.

"Please, Ramona?"

Aunt Mollye excused herself. Mom and I sat. Then, abruptly, she pointed the remote at the television and turned it on. I waited a few seconds and stood up. "You gonna watch TV?"

Mom shrugged. "I'm not doing anything else."

"Okay, then. See ya."

She turned it off. Sighed, without looking at me. And then the tears started to well in her eyes.

"Don't, Mom. Please."

"I can't help it."

"I'm going to leave if you cry."

She wiped her eyes. "Why are you treating me like this?"

"I'm not doing anything except waiting to see if we can talk to each other."

"Well, if you'd come by once in a while, if you'd call or spend the holidays with me . . ." Her voice trailed off.

"Why is it always my fault?"

She turned her gaze toward me and we stared at each other.

"Tell me, Mom. Really, I want to know. Why is it always my fault?"

For once, she looked down first. "I'm sick, Mona."

"I know."

"I can't help myself."

I didn't say anything, but my lips tightened. She shook her head at me. "You're just like your father. You think I can just snap my fingers and be okay. I didn't choose this, you know. I didn't say, 'Hey, I'd like to be bipolar, please, so I can screw up my entire life.'"

"Yeah, well, I didn't choose to be your daughter, either. So we both have some shit to deal with."

We tried to stare each other down, then her eyes teared again, and she dropped her head into her hands. I turned and looked out the window, listening as she cried. I tried to sort through the thoughts racing around my brain, but there were just too many.

"Is there a tissue?" she asked, her voice like air. I barely heard.

"Yeah. Here." I handed her the box from the table.

"I'm sorry, Mona."

"I know."

"It's hard for me."

"It's hard for me, too."

"I just don't know what I'd do if you left for good."

"How can I do that, Mom? We're family."

"Your father left."

"Well, you know what? Good. I'm glad he did. He sounds like a prick. And you know what else? I'm not him. I'm me."

"Mona—"

"I wouldn't recognize him if I fell over him. And I'm tired of you blaming me for shit I couldn't do anything about. Okay? I'm tired of it."

"Listen—"

"And I'm really sorry that you're sick, Mom. But I didn't do that either."

"I know."

"I love you. You're my mother and I love you. But I need a break sometimes, too, okay? I don't always do things right."

She didn't answer right away, just studied my face. Then she reached out her hand and I took it. "Okay."

When I finally got home that night, it was around nine. I went by Noah's first, I'm not even sure why. He was out, but Daniel and Andy were there, and Daniel's new girlfriend. I shook my head in disgust, turned around, and headed down the stairs.

"Yeah, well, you should talk," Daniel called after me, with an evil little chuckle. I whirled to answer him, but the mocking expression on his face stopped me. What the hell had I ever seen in him? I headed across the street. I could feel him watching my ass as I walked.

It all made sense in a perverse sort of way. It was just me, my karma. I fell in love at the wrong time, with the wrong people. I pissed off friends just when I needed them to be close. I made bad choices for stupid reasons (which seemed perfectly plausible the moment they presented themselves), and I slept with people I shouldn't have. I knew it, and I didn't change things. Why should I be surprised when it all backfired?

Samantha

"At first everybody helps, you know? They bring food and they clean up your house. And they all talk about 'just call.' Then they go. And you do call a few of them, maybe, or they call you, for a while. But after the first couple of months, they don't know what to say anymore. Because they're all back to their own lives, and they expect you to get back to yours." Sal chuckled wryly. "Except yours died."

At first, I hardly realized he was speaking. We were in the office, doing the bookkeeping he let me help with when I came in early. He didn't sound like himself; his voice barely raised above a whisper. I didn't dare move or even look directly at him. I didn't want him to stop. He addressed his words to the floor.

"So, after a while you think maybe you've gone a bit off the deep end, too, because you don't have nothing else to talk about except how long the nights are and how empty the house is. And nobody wants to hear it. So you keep it to yourself. You keep it to yourself and it churns around inside. Even when you try not to dwell on it, there it is. A song. Or maybe the way some stranger turns her head that reminds you. Or even a color."

He shrugged a little, and sighed. "But it's very strange. Laura knew a lot of people. They were always over to the house. She was always doing something for somebody. That's just the kind of person she was. But then she's gone, and they disappear. And you start worrying that maybe she really wasn't here all those years either. Because if she was, why aren't her friends still coming around?

"Then you start to lose her. Because nobody will talk about her, and if you mention her name, they turn all stony-faced or get mad or lecture you about 'moving on.' There's no one to remember with. So you put her away. Just like they did. Take the pictures down, move the furniture. I bought a new bed. New clothes. I even got a new set of cooking pots. But it didn't work. 'Cause, you know why? When I didn't have Laura, I couldn't have me. Because everything I am now has something to do with her."

Sal lowered his head and I thought he was fighting back tears.

"Sal . . . " I murmured, "you don't have to . . . "

But it wasn't that at all. He was chuckling. "No, no, let me finish. Let me tell you what I did." He glanced over and made one of his quirky Sal-faces. "You'll laugh."

I smiled, too. "I won't. I promise."

"Okay. See, Laura liked birds. Especially after she got sick. She sat for hours in our backyard and watched them swoop down and peck at the seed she threw out. They came right up to her. They knew she didn't mean no harm. Even the hummingbirds." I could see him picturing her, remembering. "She got this feeder, a red one. She saw it in a magazine somewhere, hummingbirds like red, so that's what she got. She filled it with sugar-water and put it out there, and pretty soon the birds showed up every day. She kept moving it closer and closer to her rocking chair. And the birds would still come. She got it right up next to her. And there they were. They'd come right up close."

He nodded and sighed.

"So, one morning, I see this hummingbird. Right outside of my bedroom window. And all of a sudden, I know what I gotta do. I get all the pictures down from the attic and put them up where they're supposed to be. I change the furniture back. And I start feeding the birds. Watching 'em. Looking for 'em wherever I go. Especially the hummingbirds. I get out the feeder and give it another coat of red. Because . . . when I see the birds, I see her. So I get to keep her, always, no matter what." He peeked over at me and smiled again. Even with all of his wrinkles, he seemed about twelve. "Sounds pretty stupid, huh?"

Mona

Noah showed up exactly when Samantha was getting home from work. I saw them both from the window, and could hear them on the way up the stairs. Or not hear them, actually, since they weren't exactly talking. Samantha opened the door and walked through and into the kitchen. Noah stood for a second in the doorway.

"Hey, Mon," he said to me, rolling his eyes at her back.

"More good news, Noah?" Samantha asked, taking juice out of the fridge.

"Well, yeah, but probably nothing you're interested in." He smiled at me and sneaked a wink. "I, uh, actually came over to get some of my stuff."

"Why don't you take it all?" she said it in a voice absolutely devoid of feeling. "Save yourself another visit."

"Sure, all right, if that's what you want." He started for her bedroom, then paused. "Wanna give me a hand?" he asked, throwing her that famous smile.

"Not even a little bit."

"Okay." He smiled over in my direction. "Mon?" I glanced over at Samantha.

"Yeah, 'Mon,' " she said. "Why don't you?" She grinned at me, but it didn't reach her eyes. "Maybe you could just put the stuff in *your* room."

"What's that supposed to mean?" I asked, ignoring Noah's smirk.

"What do you think it's supposed to mean?" She slammed down the glass she was using and grabbed her backpack from the sofa. "I'll be back in a few hours."

Noah burst out laughing when she shut the door. It wasn't a good sound. "Shit, did you tell her?"

"No, I didn't tell her."

"Well, somebody obviously did."

"I don't think so, I think she just knows stuff like that."

"Ooooh, maybe *Jules* told her."

I stopped right where I was and glared over at him. He didn't even notice, just kept shoving his T-shirts and stuff into a plastic bag. "Why did you sleep with me?"

He looked over at me and smiled. "Why do you think?"

"I thought it was because we both had our feelings hurt. Because we both needed to be comforted."

"Okay. That works." He headed toward the bathroom to get his shaving kit. I felt my whole body get cold.

"Were you trying to get back at Samantha?"

"For what?"

"I don't know. For not paying enough attention to you?"

"Mona. We had sex. It was fun. That's all."

"*What?*"

"This conversation will get you nothing but pissed off, okay? So let's just end it, shall we?" He came back into the living room and gave me a kiss on the forehead. "I really like you, Mona. I'm sorry none of this worked out the way you wanted, but . . . that's what happens sometimes."

"What am I supposed to do now? What do I say to Samantha?"

He shrugged. "Anything you want, I guess. She's *your* friend."

Samantha

The first thing I noticed was the garden; Mom's roses were blooming like never before. She was untangling the garden hose, when she saw the Jeep and froze. She looked thinner, in a healthy sort of way, and she'd cut *her* hair, too. She was wearing pants and a top I didn't remember. She smiled and took a few steps toward me.

"Sammie?"

I got out and waved, suddenly feeling shy. "Hi."

"Omigod—your hair! I almost didn't recognize you! You look wonderful. Oh, honey, you should have called, I would've made you dinner or something."

"That's okay." I came up close and she started to hug me, but it turned into one of those family hugs, the ones where you're not sure if you should but don't want to get in trouble if you don't. We walked inside. My mouth dropped open.

"Oh, right. You haven't seen the changes. I got a new couch, and I made an office in your room," she explained. "I hope that's okay."

This was too weird. Why was I even here? "Sure. Fine."

We stood smiling a second, then she pointed to the new couch. "Ahh . . . sit down. I'll get some drinks." She brought cranberry juice.

"Don't worry," I assured her, "I'll be careful." We sat grinning at each other like we'd just met or something. I lifted my glass for a toast.

"To your marriage."

"Thanks. Let's hope this one lasts."

"It will. How's everything going? Last thing you told me was that you found a place in Oakland. The old church?"

"We're still there. And everything is . . . well, it's coming along, I suppose. Oh, wait. Want to see your dress?" She jumped up and went in search of her wedding catalog, and I seriously considered bolting out the door, but she was too quick. "Here it is." We checked out her dress and mine, and even what Bruce was wearing. She was so polite, she didn't seem like my mom at all. Suddenly, she blinked and changed directions. "Oh. I ran into Sandra the other day. At the market."

"You did?"

"Sammie, she looks so . . . different. She's thin and sad . . . and I didn't know what to say."

"You didn't ignore her or anything, did you?"

"No, of course not. We talked, quite a while, actually. She asked all about you. But all I could think of was Julie. And I was so afraid I'd slip and say her name."

I took a quick deep breath. "That would've been okay, Mom."

"Oh no, honey, I wouldn't want to upset her by bringing it up."

I felt the old familiar mother-irritation and gave myself a

few seconds before speaking, so I could keep my tone gentle. "Do you think she ever forgets? Even a minute?"

"No." My mother looked at me in a way she never had. "I guess she doesn't."

"Mom, why didn't you ever go see Jules?" I didn't say it angrily. I really just wanted to know. She stared like I'd spit at her, then dropped her gaze to her lap. "I'm sorry, you don't have to tell me. It's really none of my—"

"I couldn't." She shrugged helplessly and picked up her glass. "I couldn't see her." Her eyes blinked and her mouth worked to keep her from crying. "I wanted to. I know Sandra would've come to see you. But I couldn't do it."

"Not even when Sandra invited you?"

She shook her head no. "Not everybody is as strong as you, Sammie." She glanced up, tears in her eyes. I felt as if I was seeing her for the very first time.

"I'm not strong, Mom."

"Yes, you are. You're like Sandra." She smiled and blinked a few more times. "You've always been more her kid than mine." We kept staring at each other. She reached out and touched my hand lightly. "But we don't have to talk about it right now, do we?"

"No, we don't."

"How's your job going?"

"Good. I like it. A lot."

"Bruce and I want to come down there and see you. Would you mind?"

"Not at all. I'll introduce you to Sal. He's the owner. He's old, but he's very cool."

"And how's Mona? And Noah?"

I sighed. For a second, I'd almost forgotten. "Fine, I guess. They slept together."

"*What?*" She reached for my hand. "Oh, Sammie, that doesn't seem like Mona."

"Yeah, well, I guess there's a side to her you missed."

"I'm sorry, honey. I know how shitty it feels."

I thought of my dad and Ruth, and nodded. "Pretty damn shitty, all right."

"Is that why you came over?"

I realized it was, and nodded again. "I didn't know where else to go. He's there now, with her, getting his stuff."

She sipped her juice and set the glass down on the side table. "Do you love him?"

"No." I shrugged. "I wanted to . . . but I really don't."

This strange little expression flitted across her face. "Was he your first, Sammie?"

I didn't know what to say.

"Honey, I slept with your dad when I was sixteen."

"No shit?" It was my turn for strange expressions.

"God, did I really just tell you that?" She blushed like a kid, and we both started laughing.

"It's okay. I'm glad you did."

"Oh, Sammie." She said my name with such love, then moved closer and took my hand. I looked down at my lap, and all of a sudden, I started to cry. "Oh, honey, it'll be okay. Really. You'll get over this and fall in love, and . . ."

"You know what? It isn't that, not really. It's Jules. I miss her so much."

"Do you, Sammie?"

I nodded. "I don't know what to do anymore. She was my best friend, Mommy."

My mom's eyes were wet. "She sure was, honey."

"I want her back. I want it never to have happened."

"I know." She put both of her arms around me and pulled me close. I stiffened, but just for a second, because this was right. This was exactly where I needed to be. She stroked my hair, and I sobbed.

After, I didn't know quite where to look. I sighed and sighed again, feeling empty and calm. Mom darted to the bathroom and came back with a wad of toilet paper for my nose. She sat down beside me again and took my hand. "Okay. Blow. And now, about the boy? Lose him, completely."

"I think I already did."

"Good girl."

"And Mona? Do I lose her, too?"

She shrugged. "I don't know. That's a lot harder." She sighed. "She does love you."

"She has a really strange way of showing it. Jules would never—"

"You're right. But she's not Julie."

"That's for damn sure."

"Sometimes people do stupid things, Sammie. Make big mistakes." She ran her hand over my hair. "Why don't you wait a little and see how you feel?"

Mona

Ryan and Erica were standing outside our door when I got home from work. Things had been moving so fast, I'd almost forgotten the two of them had gone to the East Coast.

"Hey you guys!" I called from my car. "How was New York? When did you get back?" I quickly checked the street; Samantha's Jeep wasn't here.

"Damn. Does she have to dress like this every day?" Ryan asked Erica, who promptly smacked him. "Teasing, Mona," he said to me. "I'm teasing."

"It was amazing," Erica said. "You'd love it there."

"Where is everybody?" Ryan asked.

"Oh, Samantha's at work, I guess."

"And Noah? And Daniel? And Andy?"

"I don't know. *You* live with them." I unlocked the front door and opened it. I took a step in, but they made no move to follow.

"We talked to them last night," Ryan said, "and they said they'd be home by now." He made a pouty boy face.

"Very attractive. God, I wonder what I see in you," Erica teased.

"How am I supposed to celebrate when nobody's around?" Ryan pouted.

I looked over at Erica, who smiled. "He just happened to get into that little masters program at Juilliard."

"Omigod! You did it! I was afraid to ask."

"We wanted to take everybody to dinner," Ryan announced. "But I guess we'll have to settle for you."

"We're moving in August," Ryan announced, after we eased ourselves into a booth at a little place we all liked down in the Haight. "A couple weeks before school starts."

"We?" I looked over at Erica.

"Don't be silly," she answered. "You think I'd let him be there all by himself?"

"Yeah," Ryan continued, "who else would do my laundry?"

"Shit, you guys. I hate this."

"You can come visit," Erica offered. "It's your kind of city. You'll love it."

Just then the food arrived. As they talked all about the various auditions Ryan had set up, and all the different schools he liked, I kept thinking how much I'd miss them, especially Erica. Ryan started telling the story of the one audition he really botched, and I laughed so hard I almost choked on my shrimp. After, we ordered coffee, and when it came, Ryan excused himself to go to the restroom. We chatted a bit about New York apartments, then Erica leaned forward over the table.

"Okay. Enough of this bullshit. Tell."

"What?"

"I've heard the rumors."

My stomach turned over all by itself. "Like . . .?"

"Like you and Sammie are fighting over Noah."

"Well, that's not exactly true . . . ."

"And you and Noah . . . uh, you know."

"Yeah." I sighed. "That part's true. Who did you talk to?"

"Noah."

"Shit. Does Ryan know?"

"Does Ryan know what?" Ryan asked, sitting back down.

"Nothing. Never mind," I said.

"He's the one who talked to him."

"Oh. Great." I muttered. "Now everybody thinks I'm a slut."

"Well, if you are," Ryan told me, "you're not the only one."

"What do you mean?" I asked. Erica shook her head at Ryan, but he ignored her.

"Noah's like a rabbit," Ryan explained. "He jumps into every hole he can find." Erica punched him in the arm, hard. "Well, he does," Ryan insisted, rubbing his arm. "We were surprised he stayed with Sammie as long as he did. And Daniel's worse," Ryan added. "Andy's the guy you should have gone for."

"Thanks for telling me."

Ryan grinned. "Anytime."

"I still feel stupid," I said.

"You should," Erica said, her voice very quiet and serious-sounding. "Because that was not okay."

Ryan jumped in. "Yo—Erica, back off now."

"Mona knows I'm telling the truth. Don't you?"

"Yeah. But . . . you haven't been living with her, Erica," I said. "You don't know how it was."

"I will if you tell me."

"All I ever wanted was to be her friend. But she just keeps pushing me away."

"And that makes it okay to sleep with her boyfriend?"

"I didn't mean to. It just happened."

"Come on, Mona."

"It's true."

"Were you two fighting?"

"No."

She gave me that big sister look.

"Okay, yeah. Shit, I don't know what you'd call it. Noah had been really mean, and I was trying to show her I was on her side. But she told me to leave her alone, and . . . oh never mind, it all sounds stupid now."

"It doesn't matter anyway. Whatever happened, you're still her best friend. You shouldn't have gone with Noah. Period. End of story."

I glared at Erica. "Yeah, well, I tried to be her best friend, and she told me her best friend was dead."

Erica caught her breath. "Oh. Okay." She glanced over at Ryan. "That's what's going on here."

"Look, you could not possibly make me feel any worse than I already do, so why don't I just go?" I started to stand. "I'm so sorry. I know I let everybody down, but—"

"Mona, sit down, please."

I didn't, but I didn't move away either.

"I just want you to recognize what's true, and what's not."

Totally out of the blue, I started to tear up. And I couldn't stop. "I do."

She put her hand out and I took it, then sat back down.

"But I don't know what happens now."

"You talk to her."

"Erica, I don't know what to say. I never know what to say."
I managed a little smile. "Which doesn't matter, anyway, because
we're not speaking. We just come and go totally on our own, like
we're at a hotel or something."

"She'll come around."

"I don't think so."

"Give her time, Mon."

"You always say that."

"Maybe because it's the only thing that works." She reached
over, like a mom, and brushed some hair out of my face. "She's
got a lot to deal with."

"Yeah. Can we please not say it again?"

"I mean Julie."

"How long has it been?" Ryan asked.

"I guess almost a year." I sighed.

"That's not very long," he added, glancing over at Erica.

"It pisses you off, doesn't it?" Erica asked.

"No."

"*Yes.*"

"Okay, maybe it does. But only because I can't figure out
what I'm supposed to do."

"Honey, there's nothing you *can* do," Erica said softly. Ryan
reached for my other hand. "There's no way to fix it. You just
have to love her and wait it through."

"For how long?"

"Who knows? Everybody's different," Ryan said.

"It's so hard. She changes. At first she wouldn't talk about it. Now that's all she does. And she cries. Shit, she cries all the time. And I sit there feeling stupid."

"Yep," Ryan said, "that's pretty much how it goes."

"I bet she knew how to talk to Julie."

"I bet she did, too," Erica continued. "But you're not her."

"No shit."

"Give her time, Mona. *Time.*" Erica spoke in a low voice. "Stay close, be honest, and give her time."

The waiter came, and we sat without talking as he delivered the bill. When he was gone, Erica slipped her arm through Ryan's.

"He used to shut me out, too."

"Yeah, I did," Ryan said, nodding. I looked from one to the other, not understanding. Both of them grinned. "You mean for once Daniel has not told my entire life story?"

I shook my head. Erica smiled a little.

"Both my parents were killed in a plane crash when I was seventeen." Ryan's tone was matter-of-fact, not emotional at all. "About two weeks before I met this girl here."

"So you hang in there with Sammie, okay?" Erica said. "It'll be worth it, I promise."

Samantha

The morning of the "anniversary," I actually got up and had breakfast and was picking up the living room before I remembered. This, after thinking about nothing else for the past two weeks. I dropped on the couch and shook my head. How could Jules be gone one whole year? Then the phone rang, and I jumped.

"It's me," Sandra said softly. "I wanted to say I love you."

"I love you, too."

"Are you . . . all right?"

"So far."

"And what are your plans today?"

"I, um, I don't know. I'm supposed to go to work. But maybe I should switch days with somebody else."

"Maybe."

"But then I'd probably just cry all day."

"Yeah. Going to work sounds good. I mean, there's nothing we can do, right?"

"Right."

"What time do you finish?"

"Oh, I guess about ten."

"Will anyone be home with you?"

"I don't know."

"Well, call if you want to. I'll be up. Oh, and Rosie says hello."

"Give her a hug for me, okay?"

That's when the normal part of the day ended. From that moment on, colors were strange and nothing looked completely real. Even the sunlight was bizarre. When I crossed the parking lot behind Malone's, the gravel sounded weird. I took some deep breaths, but it didn't much help. When I looked across the street at the huge billboard on top of the restaurant and saw Noah staring at me, fourteen feet high, I almost thought I was hallucinating. But there he was, in all his Nike splendor.

I couldn't make him look handsome anymore. He was just a jerk who'd slept with my friend. I shook my head and said out loud, "I can't believe I was with you."

"What?" Gwyneth called, stepping across the street.

"Nothing, just talking to myself."

She peered over her glasses then hooked my arm and we went into Malone's. "You've been spending too much time here, girlfriend."

"Sammie, you got seven today," Chloe called. "Gwynnie—do bar."

I nodded, got my book in place, and went to fill the sugar shakers. Then I remembered again.

"Oh," Chloe said, coming from behind. "We got a new girl coming tomorrow. Sharyn. You're gonna train her."

"Me?" I smiled at the thought.

"You're an old-timer now, lady."

* * *

"Sammie?" Sal called from the bar a half hour or so later. "You got customers, honey."

"Thanks." I hadn't seen them sit down. I focused myself and took their order, and then the lunch rush began and carried me through until almost two. Sal found me again in the kitchen, writing up my tickets.

"Okay, so what's going on?"

I sighed. "A year today."

"Ah." He absently picked up the ones I'd done and started putting them in order.

"I can't seem to get it together."

"You saw the boyfriend, too, huh? Outside?"

"Ex-boyfriend."

"Good riddance. If he had any balls, he woulda stayed around."

Sal never ceased to surprise me. I smiled at him. "Yeah. He would have, wouldn't he?"

"Look. It's none of this my business. You can say, 'Go to hell, Sal,' if I'm bothering you."

"You're not."

"Okay, so let me tell you one thing I know. It's not much."

"Okay."

"The other day, when we talked? I liked that. I don't talk to many people. You know why?"

I shook my head no.

"Most people don't know the words."

I stared for a second, thinking maybe I was still just too spaced to get it. "I'm sorry. I don't follow."

"It's like a club, see. With its own rules. You only get in when you love somebody who dies."

"Oh," I muttered, but I didn't really understand.

"It changes you, having death be so close. You see things different than before. And after a while, you know stuff. But you can't explain it to anybody outside the club. They may want to help and they might even be willing to listen, but they won't get it. Like the boyfriend. You can't talk to him, because he don't know. He might want to. But he can't. Nobody can, until it happens to them." He stood. "Now you go home."

"But I've got the dinner shift, too."

"I'll cover."

"It might be easier to just work all day."

"There is no easy, Sammie."

"No, I guess not."

"Go home. Look at her pictures. Play some music you both liked. Go someplace that reminds you of her. Find a hummingbird."

Mona

Samantha rang the buzzer by habit, I was sure, since neither one of us had been using our old signal recently. We'd barely been talking, and when we did, we were so polite, it made me want to puke. I heard her racing up the stairs. She gasped, startled, when she opened the door and saw me.

"Shit!" she exclaimed, startled. "You scared me."

"Sorry."

"That's okay. What are you doing home?"

"They're painting the office suite." I was startled, too. It was the most we'd said to each other since the night Noah moved his stuff.

"Oh. Cool." She flew past into her room and reappeared in a blue T-shirt and her "comfy" jeans, the dance bag over her shoulder. With an evil little smile on her face, she held up a pair of brand new Nikes.

"Look what Noah forgot."

For a second, our eyes connected the way they used to. "Whoa. Those are the two-hundred-dollar ones."

"Yeah." She smiled. "Do you think we should take them over?"

"Actually, maybe we could just leave them in front. I'm sure he'll see 'em and pick 'em up."

"Good idea. Oh, but wait. You don't think somebody might steal them?"

"Samantha! In this neighborhood?"

"You're right. Silly me." She headed for the door. "Bye. Gotta run."

"Samantha . . . "

"Yeah?"

"Never mind. You're in a hurry. Maybe later we can talk?"

"Yeah. Okay. Maybe later we can."

Samantha

It was a first. Jules and I had visited "our" place up past the forts, on the hills overlooking San Francisco, at least two hundred times. No one was ever there, until now. Two kids, a boy and a girl, sat in a red pickup truck, smoking pot and blasting white rap. I felt punched; I wanted to scream at them. I needed a place to listen to my tape, and with Mona home, this was my only other choice. For a moment, I didn't know what to do. I was ready, right now this minute. But who knows if I would be this time tomorrow. I thought briefly about calling the cops on the kids.

Then I remembered Sal's "club."

Sandra opened the door after just two knocks. I was startled—she was very thin, and she obviously hadn't been dyeing her hair. There was a ton of gray.

"Yes?" she said, and I realized she hadn't seen me with short hair. Then she gasped and opened her arms, wide. The hug lasted a long time.

"I have something I want you to listen to," I said quietly, when we finally pulled apart. I held up the tape. "It's from Jules."

Sandra blinked, twice, then took a deep breath. "I don't understand."

"It's a tape from Jules. I just found it. I want you to listen to it with me."

"Wait, slow down, please. Come in. What do you mean, a tape from Jules?"

I put it in her hand. "She made it for me. It was in my dance bag, and I haven't been dancing, and . . ."

Sandra stared at it and started to tear. She handed it back. "Oh God. I don't know, Sammie. I don't think so."

"Please? I can't do it by myself."

"No. I'm not . . . I couldn't."

"If it's awful, we'll stop it."

"I can't."

"Please?"

"I don't know."

"*Please?* You said we should try to find her."

Sandra nodded and sighed again. "Wait a minute. I have to sit down." Finally, she smiled at me. "Okay. I'm all right. Let me see." She took the tape and gently turned it over. "It says 'For Sam Only.'"

"I know. But I . . . " I shook my head helplessly.

She looked in my eyes for a long moment before answering. "Okay, Sammie. I'll try. But we may have to turn it off."

"All right."

"Where should we sit?"

"By the stereo."

"It's not working. Wait a minute, Rosie got a little tape

recorder for Christmas." Sandra went to her room and came back several minutes later, shaking her head. "I can't find it."

"We could go in the Jeep."

"Hold on, maybe Julie still has hers." She headed toward Jules's room. I followed and was amazed. It was just exactly as I remembered; I felt like she could come waltzing in, any minute, toss her dance bag on the bed—. Sandra saw me looking.

"I know. I can't bring myself to change anything." I nodded, because I understood. Still, my heart was pounding as we went inside. For a second, I thought I'd freak, but being there was all right. Familiar. And somehow, good. The pictures made me hurt, but I liked them. That was us. We were together. "Here." Sandra pulled out a small cassette recorder, plugged it in and handed it to me. We both sat down on Jules's bed.

"Hold on, something's in here already." I slid out another cassette, identical to mine, except this one said: "For Mom and Dad. Please listen together."

"Oh God," Sandra murmured as she took it. I scanned the drawer where the player had been, and brought out one more. "For my Rosie."

Sandra's face did the strange little dance it performed when she wasn't letting herself cry out loud. She nodded and looked over at me.

"I can't believe it. I never looked in there." She started to really cry. "Oh, God. Oh, my baby girl. I should have known, Sammie. I should've known." She almost smiled, then she looked away. It took a few minutes for her to get herself under control. "Okay. I'm okay." She managed a smile. "Shall we start?"

Jules

"Hi, Sam. It's me . . . "

I heard Sandra suck in air the same way I had when I'd first heard her voice. I got chills.

"I'm making this tape for you. I'm not exactly sure why, 'cause I see you all the time. But guess what—I'm not sure of anything anymore. Except—wait—we need background music . . . dum da da dum dum da daaaaa! *I've got cancer."* She said it with a huge dramatic delivery.

"Stupid word, don't you think? CAN—CER. Cancer, cancer, cancer. I'm a cancer-dancer. Go ahead, say that six times in a row! But don't worry, it's not really true. It couldn't be. It's way too much like a soap: Girl Gets Pain and Finds Out It's Lymphoma. Then maybe in the next scene, some uncle I never met will leave me a billion dollars. See what I mean? But anyway. The tape. I'll do it as long as I can." She giggled. *"Oops. Bad choice of words. What I meant is when I remember, I'll talk. Okay?"*

The tape clicked and ran for a second before it clicked again. Jules's voice sounded tired. And pissed.

"'Everything You Ever Wanted to Know About Chemotherapy' by Juliana I-Hate-This-Shit Michaels. Ready? Okay. First, you get

hooked up to a needle that burns like hell. Then you throw up. That's entertaining. Food smells like caca. Your father pretends nothing's happening. Your little sister walks around pissed because she can't watch the TV, and your mother never sleeps. You, however, sleep all the time. Your friends don't call. Except you, Sam, of course. People say incredibly stupid things. And the best part? Your hair falls out. Oh yes. That's my favorite. You get to be a sixteen-year-old bald-headed freak who can't do anything at all for herself. It's very pleasant. You should try it sometime. You'd love it. Not."

Click. A pause. And her voice began again, a bit less sarcastically.

"How do you do this? You actually managed to get my sorry self out of bed and out of the house! I cussed you, I talked about your mother (like you care, right), I even tried to physically hurt you. But you are one stubborn shit. And you know what? It was okay. No, what am I saying? It was amazing! You made me laugh all night, Sam. God, I love you. When this is all over, we'll . . . well, we'll do something so . . . so incredibly spectacular . . . no one will be able to stand it.

Sandra reached over and took my hand. Both of us tried smiling, but it didn't quite work. Jules's voice, when she next came on, changed dramatically. It was hard for her to speak. She didn't finish her sentences, but took long deep breaths in between.

"I don't know what day it is, Sam. I just know it's been a long time since I did this tape thing. All I do now is lay here and . . . have strange dreams and then . . . get hooked up to that poison and throw up. But you came to see me, didn't you? I think it was my birthday.

Didn't you come to see me? I don't know for sure. Everything's too hard." She started to cry. *"I can't . . . I really can't . . . stand this anymore."*

Click.

"It's Christmas. Where's Santa, do you think? If you run into him, mention I'm in the hospital." There was a pause, but no click. *"I don't know if I'll be doing this tape anymore. There doesn't seem much point."*

Click. Sandra looked over with a question in her face. I shrugged a little.

"I don't know. Let's wait."

A second later, Jules was back, sounding a bit more like her old self.

"Okay—guess what? I have a life again! I'm dancing! Well, maybe not dancing *dancing, but at least I took class! I even tried a bit of rehearsal. You don't know how long I've wished for this. You wouldn't believe how much I want to* really *dance. I should've stopped that chemo shit a long time ago. I'm even back at school. Maybe maybe maybe maybe . . . just maybe, everything's going to be okay."*

Click. And her voice was hard to describe.

"It's back. The same, Sam, maybe worse. I'm not telling you or anyone, not yet. First I have to do the concert. Then we'll see. Hey, we talked today, at school, just for a second. You have a boyfriend now and you looked so pretty." A brief pause, but no click. *"I feel so left out."*

Click.

"The pain got too awful. I had to tell my mom. Dr. Bitch Conner was thrilled. She wanted to say, 'I told you so.' But she didn't." There

was a very brief pause, like a breeze going through. *"She did tell Mom I'm terminal."* Sandra took a deep, quick breath. *"My mom said to keep it to herself. They don't know I heard."*

I reached over and put my hand on Sandra's. Click. This time Jules was crying. Softly, like a kitten.

"My hair fell out this morning. She said it wouldn't, but she lied! She fucking lied!"—a sigh—*"Oh, Sam. I don't know how to do this anymore. There's nothing left."*

There was no click, just a long silence. When she came back on, her voice was tight and strained.

"What did I do? Was I an asshole or something? Why did I have to get sick? Why couldn't it be Rosie or you or my mom? Why did it have to be me?" Another long pause, but we could hear her breathing. *"Sorry. I'm sorry—that was mean. I don't really want you to be sick. I just wish I . . ."* she sighed, *"I wish somebody would understand."*

She started to cry softly again, then turned off the machine. A second later, it clicked again.

"Hi, Sam. I got to dance in the show. I tried to be good . . . I tried so hard . . . but I could barely finish my dances. I didn't even get to bow with you, after 'Little Girls.' I wanted to. I just couldn't walk out there. Then I yelled at Rosie. Can you believe it? The one person who isn't pretending . . . the one person who really doesn't *know."*

She paused.

"You do. So do my mom and dad. The kids in the company. Even the people in the audience. You all look right through me like I'm already gone. You just don't say it. But guess what. I have to. 'Cause I know it now, inside me. You ready? I'm going to die, Sam. Pretty soon, probably. I'm going to die."

When she started speaking again, her voice had changed. She sounded like a little girl.

"I need you, Sam. I'm scared. I need you so bad."

Sandra and I glanced briefly at each other, but neither one of us could speak. In the next entry, Jules's voice was almost an echo. We had to stop a few times to rewind and listen again.

"Hey, Sam I Am. It's close, I think. It hurts a lot, but it's a different sort of pain . . . separate from me. I can stand it. And anyway, if I can't, I have all this morphine, right?"—a pause—*"And I think I'm ready. That's what you have to know. I'm ready."* Another pause, this one longer—*"I want to leave now, Sam. It's time.*

"I wish I could tell you this in person. And I wish you could say, 'I know, Jules. I know you have to die. But it'll be okay, because I'll be here, any time you need me.'" She made a little sound, like a chuckle. *"I mean, what if I screw it all up?"* —a pause, another little chuckle—*"Don't worry. I won't. I mean, how hard can it be? Everybody does it. Oh, and I'm going to the banquet tomorrow. I have to give you this tape."*

I looked over at Sandra and she shrugged. I reached to turn off the machine just as Jules's voice came on one last time.

"Hey, Sam, I have to say good-bye now. I love you. I love you more than you will ever ever know. Remember that. Remember I'm your One and Only. Remember you're a dancer—and you always will be. How could you not? You're my Other Self. Remember you are the most amazing, incredible friend anyone could want. You give me so much. Even when I'm sick and scared and awful, you make me laugh. You held me in so many ways. You never even knew it."

"Oh, my Sam. I'd stay if I could, for you. But I'm so tired, so unbelievably tired. It's just too hard. I have to go. I want to. Don't cry

too much, all right? And go see my family. Tell Rosie—tell her that I love her, will you? And I'm sorry I wasn't a better sister. And tell my mom and dad . . . I don't know, it'll sound strange, but tell 'em I'm ready. That I'm not sad. I'm not even scared, not anymore. I know stuff I can't even begin to explain.

"One more thing. Really important. Promise promise, Sam. I mean it. I want you to dance for me . . . As long as you can . . . As hard as you dare.

"Bye."

Samantha

The class was in the middle of their combination when I sneaked in the side door to watch. Linda jerked her head in my direction, no doubt to yell at whoever had interrupted her work, but then she saw it was me. Her mouth stayed open a second, then she smiled. I smiled back. The dancers looked so young, though I knew they were only a year or so behind me and Jules.

"Hi, Sammie."

"Hi. Sorry to interrupt."

"No, it's fine. Come on in." She glanced back at the class. "From the top, please, girls."

I shook my head and smiled. "I'll come back."

"Promise?"

"Yes."

She nodded and blew me a kiss.

From there, I went by Tam High. I parked up on the hill where we used to go to talk when we skipped class. I went down to the campus and walked to all our places, taking a moment in each to remember something we'd said or done. I kept waiting for Jules, but she didn't come. I drove through Mill Valley and then halfway up the mountain, to the playground we'd hike up to before we had cars. I climbed up the wooden structure in the corner, and hunkered down in the corner, amazed at how small it seemed. This was where I'd told Jules about my mom and dad getting divorced.

The sun was setting, and the sky over the mountain turned that brilliant orange-fire gold, outlining the peaks and the weird little bubble building on the very top. The color slowly drained away, and the same picture presented itself in shades of blues, then in black and gray. I had to force myself to move. There was one last trip—up the freeway, like we'd always done any time the world got to be too much. As cold as it was, I took the top off the Jeep and I dug way down to the bottom of my glove box for the Doors, John Lennon, and Billie Holiday. They were Jules's tapes, and I'd kept them tucked away all this time. One by one, I blasted her favorite songs and sang along at the top of my lungs.

But no long hair whipped my face, and no familiar laugh came from the other side of the Jeep. I had the costumes, the sets, the music and the choreography . . . but there was no dancer girl. I could play her voice and I could remember stuff . . . but she wasn't there. There was no more Jules, not anywhere. I'd have to figure out how to do the rest of my life without her.

I sighed. I couldn't—*wouldn't*—go back to feeling nothing. That was worse even than the pain.

Mona

Samantha came into my room, I don't know how late—but it had to be well after midnight. I was reading. I'd heard her key in the door, but even though we'd actually talked this afternoon, I didn't call out. My body tensed. I waited. She knocked lightly and pushed open the door.

"Hi." Her voice was very soft.

"Hi." I sighed, not being able to stop myself.

"Can I come in?"

"Sure."

She stood just inside the room and spoke quietly, no real feeling in her voice. "It was a year today." I looked close—her face had changed. Something was different, in the eyes.

"Julie?"

"Mm-hm."

"Damn."

"Yeah. I went to see her mom. And then I drove all over, to all our places." She tried to smile, but it didn't come out so good. "Stupid, huh?" She turned, slightly, like she was getting ready to leave.

As usual, I didn't know what to say. She wasn't ready to leave, I could tell that, but once again, forever, I was helpless. I blurted the first thing that came into my mind. "You could stay here if you want."

"Maybe for a while?"

"Sure."

She came over to the bed and sat down on the end, her head hanging forward. She ran her hand through her hair, and a tear slipped out and dropped on her lap. Then another, and another. I scooted over close and put my arms around her. I didn't say a word, just held her while she cried. Her pain was so enormous, her tears so utterly helpless; all I could do was stay close and hope that being there could ease it even just a little. I felt my own tears start. I don't know how long we sat there, but finally, she was able to stop. I wiped her face with my T-shirt.

She glanced over at me and smiled. "Snotted ya, huh?"

"Yeah. Who cares."

"Sorry."

"It doesn't matter." We were quiet for a few minutes. When she next looked up at me, she took my breath away. She looked like a scared little girl.

"I miss her. I really really miss her."

"I know."

She stared straight into my eyes for a second and shook her head just a bit. "No, you don't, Mona. You don't know. You really don't."

I stared right back. Her voice was gentle and totally kind. She wasn't pushing me away. She was simply telling me a truth. I nodded, still crying a little, and ignored the pang inside.

"She was part of me; she knew what I was thinking and feeling."

I nodded again. I wanted to take her hand, but I couldn't quite do it.

"I used to call her My One and Only." She sniffed and smiled, even laughed a little. "That sounds really dumb when I say it out loud."

"No, it doesn't."

"I was her Other Self." Her mouth quivered and the tears started to flow again. "So when she died, I couldn't . . . I didn't know how to even live anymore."

"Samantha, I—"

"No, wait, I'm not done." She turned toward me and took my hand in both of hers. "I want you to know something. You helped me, a lot. From the very beginning of that stupid English class. You helped. Even when you didn't know you were doing it. You made me laugh!" She sniffed and then blew her nose and managed to stop the tears. Then she reached out and took my hand. "I think what I'm trying to say is I want us to be friends."

I started crying again. "I am so sorry."

"I know."

"I'd do anything to change it."

"It doesn't matter now."

"I really love you."

"I love you, too."

"I don't want to move out."

"Me, either."

"Do you think we really can be friends?" I blew my nose, too. "Maybe start over or something?"

"I think we could try."

"Okay."

"It might take a while."

"I know."

Her eyes twinkled a little, not just from the tears. "'Cause you are still an asshole, you know."

I smiled. "If I'm an asshole . . . "

"Yeah, yeah." She stood up. "Me, Shithead. It'll make a great TV show: *Shithead and Asshole*."

"Hey—maybe we can get Noah and Daniel to play the title roles."

Samantha

Five days later, for my nineteenth birthday, I took myself out to breakfast. I ordered pancakes and toasted Jules silently with my milk. I wrote a special invitation to Rosie to come spend the night at our apartment. My mom and dad each called later in the morning, and I actually made plans with them both, though who could say if my dad would keep his. Sandra called, too, and Linda, and then, of all people—Colleen. She was coming home for the summer, and I promised I'd let her know when we could get together. Mona hinted at some incredible midnight dinner after work, complete with cake and ice cream. I saw my Lady out the window and she gave me a shy little wave. And I didn't have to be at Malone's until four. Which was good, because I had something very important I wanted to do.

I found a parking space right in front and walked up the stairs, my heart pounding like I was going to jump out of a plane or something. I shifted the bag on my shoulder. *It's just dance class,* I yelled inside my head; *you've been doing this your entire life.*

But I'd been doing it with Jules.

"For Volovochev's?" the girl at the desk asked.

"Yes, please." I handed her my money.

"It's Ballet Four," she warned, glancing at my obviously unworked-out body.

"I know."

She gave me a receipt and I followed her directions to the dressing room. *This is ridiculous*, I thought, as I felt myself break out in a nervous sweat. The girls changing around me chatted on about this and that; it was just another class, and they'd probably been dancing together for a while. Except for an initial curious glance, no one acknowledged me at all. I followed the group to the studio and waited a second until everybody found their places. I didn't want to take somebody's favorite spot. Feeling almost like I'd pass out, I went to the barre and faced right, glancing around. This was not the studio I'd danced in with Jules, but everything was familiar—the mirrors, barres, scarred floor, rosin boxes.

Volovochev walked in. He was different than I remembered; older, with a bony face framed by incredible eyebrows and a huge mane of white hair. He carried a cane and his limp was more pronounced. His gaze rested on me a second and he squinted a bit, as if he were trying to place me, but he didn't say anything. Then he pounded his cane twice on the floor, and the dancers took second position.

"Four demi, relevé, four grande, and stretch. Repeat first, fourth, fifth." He pounded again and the accompanist began to play.

"Prepare, one and two." It was Linda's voice I heard in my head as I lifted my arms up and out to second, and began the pliés. Immediately, my muscles protested; it had been more than a year since I'd last danced, and even this most basic of warm-ups was taxing. Volovochev walked by and jabbed softly at my ribcage.

"Close," he murmured and I pulled in and up. He walked on. Inside, my soul smiled. I'd come home.

I did the entire barre—unlike the first time I'd been here. My legs were actually shaking when we were done. A final stretch and slow splits, then out to center for the *port de bras* and *adage*. After that, the variation. It was murder, fast and precise—exactly the kind of combination I used to love. But you needed balance and strength to dance it well—which only comes with time and work. I silently cussed myself for not taking a lower level class.

Volovochev ignored me the first few times through. Then he stood to my left and watched. I faltered twice, my *attitude* was not at all where it should have been, and though I went for the triple pirouette, I fell out of it after two.

"Again." Volovochev barked and the music started. I did better this time, not falling out. He took my leg in arabesque and lifted it three inches more. "Good. There is where it should be. Again. You people," he gestured with his cane at the group, "watch."

To my horror, my face turned beet red as I took fifth and the music began. This time, again, I missed the pirouette entirely.

"No. You need hold, here." He jabbed at my ribs again. "And here." He flicked the upper part of my butt. "Go."

I nodded and took fifth, and felt the tears long before they found their way to my eyes. This was always the difference between Jules and me—she pushed through and I gave up. I was ready to leave now. I should never have come. Jules was the dancer. Volovochev pounded the cane, and the music began.

Jules is in fifth, at the barre, concentrating so hard, the sweat runs down her face. Her wig's slipped a little, but she doesn't notice.

"No! You must pull up! Start again!"

We hold the attitude, close together, at the beginning of "Little Girls." Jules is shaking with the effort, with what used to be so very easy . . . and when we turn upstage, I see her tears.

I took fifth again, and concentrated, and bit back the tears, and tried as hard as I knew how, until my muscles were screaming and the other girls were turning away, embarrassed for the way Volovochev was pushing, or maybe for me not being able to get it right. My entire body glistened with sweat. He shook his head and leaned on the cane.

"You cry?" he asked.

I shook my head no, and tried to quickly wipe my eyes.

"I see. I think, 'Ah, dancer!'" he murmured with a small shake of the head, his deep brown eyes boring into me. "But you not dancer."

"I want you to dance for me . . ."

"Yes, I am," I whispered, barely heard.

"No. You not work hard. Dancer work, always. Never give up. So enough." He turned toward the rest of the class. "Okay. Everybody now. Pirouette. From second, then fifth . . . "

" . . . *as long as you can . . . "*

"Could I try it just once more?" I asked, slightly above a whisper.

" . . . *as hard as you dare."*

He didn't look at me. "For why? You cannot do."

Jules and I face each other across the studio. We're ten. The gauntlet is thrown, and I know I've met someone I'll know for the rest of my life.

We run laughing along the ocean. "It's talking, Sam, do you hear it?"

I'm crying; my father's just left. She holds me and strokes my hair. "I love you. Don't worry. I'm here."

We both reach for that imaginary ribbon, and as her hand closes around it, she turns to me, and smiles.

I ask anyway. From between her parents, she whispers that awful word.

I hold her, her body so small, I think she might break.

"Dance for me . . . "

The seagull stares, and stares.

"As long as you can . . . "

And then it nods.

"He called me a dancer."

"As hard as you dare . . . "

I crossed to where Volovochev stood and stared directly into his eyes. "Please."

He stared back, a long moment, then, with a tap of his cane, started the pianist playing, and folded his arms across his chest to watch.

I took a long slow breath. The waves and the sky, Jules's face and the seagull merged inside me; here, in a dance class with people I didn't know, without Jules . . . and forever and ever—because of her. Everything we ever did or talked about, dreamed of, smiled at; every plié, every tear, every single moment of laughing, hoping, fighting . . . I had it all. I had Jules. She was inside me. So, now, finally, once again, I had myself. And as long as I was here, in the world, she would be, too.

Her face, laughing.

Her hand, holding mine.

Her voice, telling the story of pain, joy, long nights, dark things, and understanding.

Promise *promise???*

I listened and raised my arms and began to dance.

Acknowledgments

Love and thanks to my early readers, Colleen & Lew Ross and Mollye Hurwin; to Laura Clark and Kelly Kagan; to Ramona Rae Rose, who lent me her name and "teen expertise"; to editor Sharyn November and literary agent Bonnie Nadell; to Alpin Hong, whose courage inspires me; to Stephen Sondheim, whose music continues to help me survive giants; and to my dear friend and writing mentor, Carol McKeand, who keeps me honest.

Love and my heart to soulmate and husband, Gene Hurwin, who reads everything and hates when I make him cry—and to my very wise and beautiful daughter, Frazier Malone—who is, of course, my reason for everything.

In memory of Cathy Moore, Cliff Smith, Leticia Crestejo,
Miriam Hurwin, Kaleo Bright, Cathy Williams,
—and my dad.

Davida Wills Hurwin is also the author of *A Time for Dancing* (an ALA Best Book for Young Adults). She teaches theater at Crossroads School for Arts and Sciences, and lives in Southern California with her husband, Gene, and their daughter, Frazier Malone.